THE LIFE
OF THE MIND

Christine Smallwood

THE LIFE
OF THE MIND

Europa
editions

Europa Editions
8 Blackstock Mews
London N4 2BT
www.europaeditions.co.uk

A catalogue record for this title is available from the British Library
ISBN 978-1-78770-345-2

Smallwood, Christine
The Life of the Mind

Book design by Emanuele Ragnisco
www.mekkanografici.com

Cover image: Elisabetta Sirani, *Portia wounding her thigh*
© Alamy Stock Photo

Prepress by Grafica Punto Print – Rome

Printed and bound in Great Britain by Clays Ltd, Elcograf S.p.A.

CONTENTS

The End of March - 13

The Next Day - 42

Five Days Later - 71

A Few Weeks Later - 102

Saturday Night, The Next Week - 159

Ten Days Later - 183

Acknowledgments - 201

About the Author - 203

For my friends

THE LIFE
OF THE MIND

The End of March

Dorothy was taking a shit at the library when her therapist called and she let it go to voicemail. The therapist was calling because Dorothy, who at this moment was rereading the flyer for student health services taped to the wall above the receptacle for used feminine-hygiene products, had left a voicemail at eleven o'clock last night canceling today's session. It wasn't that the miscarriage was such a big deal or that she was broken up in grief about it; it was that she hadn't told her therapist she was pregnant, and didn't want to have a whole session about her tendency to withhold. In the asymmetrical warfare of therapy, secrets were a guerrilla tactic. Not that Dorothy had been plotting to keep things to herself. She wasn't the plotting type.

It was day six, and she was still bleeding. Not the unceasing hemorrhage of the first ten hours—now it was thick, curdled knots of string, gelatinous in substance. In most cases of gestational stall it wasn't necessary to intervene; the body knew to spontaneously expel its failures. Perhaps that accounted for the trauma in other women's accounts—the element of surprise. *You will know not the day nor the hour!* In her case the body had held on, deferential, waiting for her to clear her schedule. The result was less than a trauma and more than an inconvenience. She would never know exactly when it had happened—when it had stopped happening—only that she had persisted for some time idly believing that she was persisting, her body busy fulfilling its potential like some warehouse or shipping center. How typical of her not to know something was over when it was over. And how typical that it was proving more difficult to extricate herself from the dead-end pregnancy, the halted progression, than it had been to become pregnant in the first place. Her womb would not let go. The contractions had needed two Cytotec suppositories before they would even start. Misoprostol was the drug's generic name, the same one they gave you for a medication abortion. But when she did it, when she self-administered the uterine evacuation, terminating a—what was it, exactly? What did you call it when a life stopped developing, but didn't end?

TESTS GOT YOU STRESSED? the flyer quizzed. DON'T DESPAIR. TEXT TO TALK IT OUT. A sad stick figure in one corner, a smiling stick figure in the other. KILL YOURSELF, someone had written in green ink above the smiler. STOP THE HATE, someone else had written alongside, in letters so small they seemed afraid to draw attention to themselves. Then the hand in green ink had returned to draw a drooling penis with a thick beard and a natty top hat. Dorothy wondered if she had taught any of these students. It was possible.

She hadn't intended to lie to her therapist—if an omission even counted as a lie. Dorothy hadn't been pregnant for very long, but she had been pregnant long enough to understand that unless she was very tactical in her behavior, her body and what she did with it, what she put into it, would be a matter of community interest. Maybe pregnancy changed the body from a private to a public thing, or maybe it exposed the nature of the body as already public. Whatever it was, it was something she wanted to talk out with her therapist, except when it was on her tongue to do so, the therapist had interrupted a warm-up story that Dorothy was telling about her boyfriend, Rog, to remark that he was "a keeper." Dorothy saw at once that after the language of "keeping" had been introduced into the room, it would be impossible to keep it from becoming attached to the pregnancy, to define the pregnancy in terms of a keeping or a not-keeping, when in fact Dorothy was not ready to talk about retention, even as a future decision toward which she was inevitably hurtling, and so she, driven into a cul-de-sac by a linguistic overdetermination that would have been rich material if she only could have borne it, said nothing.

The therapist had apologized for calling Rog "a keeper."

"Who you keep is up to you, not me," she had said, gazing earnestly into Dorothy's eyes, willing her into compliance, but Dorothy disagreed. What was this American fixation on doing it yourself? Wasn't she in therapy so that someone would tell her what to do? What use was expert knowledge, the years paid out acquiring experience, if it was kept in reserve, hoarded like canned goods, while the masses stumbled about, starving and ignorant? Voicing these opinions only worsened the situation; they spent the rest of the session processing the incident, and when Dorothy returned the following week, she couldn't find her way back, couldn't justify not having confessed the pregnancy right away. Time had intervened; an innocent delay had become a falsehood. So she kept it to herself. And kept it the next week. And again the week after that. And then she "lost" the pregnancy—misplaced it, like a keychain—and now she thought she might keep it forever, so awful was the thought of returning to the beginning of the story, now that she was in its end.

Martin Luther thought up the "95 Theses" while he was on the toilet.

Dorothy couldn't remember where she had read that.

She wiped, examined her fingernails, wiped again. She wiped back to front. She knew this was incorrect, but she had been doing it her whole life, and there are habits one gives up on breaking.

The toilet didn't have an automatic flush, so Dorothy could

sit for hours if she chose and never be sprayed with water. She opened her phone and scrolled back through her photos. There was an old one that she liked a great deal, of Rog playing with his brother's dog. Rog was at peace, and the dog's face was a rictus of joy. Rog had dumb long hair then. The dog in the photo was now dead. It had died of a mysterious ailment that manifested as a sudden explosion of tumorous growths all over its long body. Dorothy remembered stroking the dog the day before they put it under. It was like stroking a sock filled with gravel.

Dorothy did not frequent the large women's room by the water fountain, with its row of six open-bottomed stalls under which could be passed fistfuls of paper or whatever else a person required. She used the single-occupancy bathroom by the critical-theory reading room. The bathroom was large—designed to be wheelchair accessible, though everyone used it—and smelled faintly of disinfectant. She bent over and took from her bag a small bottle of peppermint oil and sniffed.

The handle of the bathroom door shuttled back and forth.

"I'm in here!" Dorothy called.

If she had opted for the in-office procedure, they would have vacuumed her clean. But she had wanted to bleed at home. It had seemed less official that way. She hadn't known how degrading the dribble would be. Dorothy was starting to fear it might never end; that until the last of her days, whenever she wiped, the tissue would come back bloody and brown. She didn't have much experience with blood, abscesses, sores, things of that nature. She had never broken a bone or needed stitches. Once she saw a cyst explode. It happened in college. Her roommate, Alyssa, had developed a soft lump on her elbow that over several weeks expanded like a balloon being pumped with water until one afternoon she bent her arms to put her hair in a pony and streams of white confetti burst out, decorating the books, pencils, etc., on her desk, as well as her denimed lap, with foamy spray. Dorothy ran from the room in horror, but Alyssa, fascinated by the materials of the body, took photographs.

Alyssa had a "natural" approach to life. Dorothy had learned this early in their friendship, when during a wild party for spring fling they fell into an embrace. Dorothy would estimate the number of rum-based drinks she enjoyed that evening at five. She and Alyssa kissed and groped and were soon scouring the building, whose name was Trotter, for a room with a door, pursuing like two moles the feeling of being shut in, unobservable, burrowed. The classrooms were locked, but the spacious single-occupant bathroom on the ground floor was open.

In her memory the floor sparkled cold and blindingly white, as did the lavatory's other features: the walls, the sink, the toilet, the light, the grout that separated and conjoined the tiles. There was a word for that, "cleaving," for what joined together and pushed apart. Alyssa jerked down her pants, exposing a tangle of hair, and reached a hand inside. She pulled out a maroon latex cup that came to a point like a nipple. It was called, Dorothy remembered, a Keeper. Hippies used them, vegans, people like that. In her drunken enthusiasm Alyssa was clumsy and spilled the blood. It left a trail like drizzled syrup on her blond leg, across the clean tiled floor. Alyssa's reaction was merry. She tossed the cup into the sink and wiped the blood away with the cheap single-ply toilet paper, leaving smudges everywhere, and without pausing to apologize showed Dorothy how to form her first two fingers into a rod and ram it back and forth in the place where the keeper had been, and as Dorothy did this for Alyssa she was overcome with a feeling of desolation and loneliness and fatigue. Dorothy wasn't used to being so active, sexually speaking. She preferred lying down on something soft and warm like a bed and letting someone else do the ramming.

The knocking at the door turned harassing.

"I'm in here!" Dorothy called again.

While the footsteps receded down the hall, she listened to her voicemail. The therapist had a pleasant phone voice. "I'm sorry that you're not feeling well," she said. "Rest up and I'll see you next week." In the pauses between the words hung no distrust. Before she could put her phone away, Rog texted to ask how she was feeling. She wrote back, "Still bleeding." She flushed. She inspected her fingernails.

Thinking back on it now, Dorothy marveled at how clean the Trotter bathroom had been. Her own finger had been the dirtiest thing there. Other than the spatter, which was not really so big—the Keeper cup could hold only thirty milli-liters, less than a shot of liquor—there was not a speck of dirt or grime anywhere on any part of the toilet. Not the lid or the lip or the rim or the trunk. The library toilet was similarly pris-tine. You could lie down with your face pressed up against the ceramic base and it would be incommodious but not repul-sive. But Dorothy's toilet at home was always dirty, and cov-ered in her own hair. Some days it seemed like Dorothy's hair was threaded with magnets and the toilet was burnished in steel, the way they attracted each other. And how does she have any hair left at all, she thought, considering how it clogs the drain and collects around the edges of the bath mat, how it fills the crooks of her fingers when she tugs on the ends in concentration, how so much of it has been falling out, day after day after day?

No one was waiting outside the bathroom door. Dorothy dipped her head to the water fountain, which was clogged by a piece of chewing gum. Some water spilled over the side, and she stepped back to stay dry. Other people had jobs that kept them well away from gum-lined troughs. They had seltzer machines, snack dispensers, expense accounts. The gum had once been blue or green and was now a sickly pale. The fountain water was lukewarm. It would have been better to have drunk from the bathroom tap.

There were, to be sure, other things in therapy that Dorothy had kept to herself, questions that lingered unasked, doubts she had failed to articulate. For three years running they had been meeting every Tuesday (save a New Year's holiday and the thirty-one days of August) in the stuffy fifteenth-floor studio on Central Park West, with its treetop view and standard-issue décor: African masks, Oriental rugs, afghan throws, South American flutes. Dorothy was comforted by the therapist's warmth and womanliness, her aging but elastic skin, the way she clucked and wiped her hands like someone who had seen it all and intended to save you the trouble of seeing it for yourself. Still, more and more it worried Dorothy to have entrusted her mental health to one who made such little effort against the tide of cliché. It was one thing for problems—even solutions—to be unoriginal; another for presentation.

When the worrying got too intense, Dorothy had a choice of palliatives arrayed in pouncing distance of the saggy patient sofa: stress balls, beads, figurines for rubbing and handling, various-size pillows for pounding and embracing, and the eternal tissue box, draped in its hand-knitted elephant-gray cover. The box was always full. The therapist must be keeping watch on the box's levels. Dorothy respected her attention to detail. Fullness, plenitude, preparedness, a material well of empathy—excellent clinical values all. But where did the therapist hide the half-full boxes? Or did she cram new tissues into the same old box between sessions? How old was the box, and how old were the tissues at the deepest, most archaeological substratum, and what might happen if Dorothy had a particularly lachrymal session and made it all the way down to the bottom?

She took the elevator down to the stacks. She was not sorry

she had skipped the session, but she missed seeing her therapist. She wondered what she was doing with her free hour. Not long ago Dorothy had started seeing a second therapist, in whom she confided her doubts about the first therapist. This was only a temporary situation. Dorothy wasn't a millionaire.

The buzz of fluorescence increased in volume as Dorothy got farther from the elevator. One of the overhead light panels was refusing to go quietly from this world. The agonized industrial hum pushed into Dorothy's head until she felt it emanate outward from within rather than inward from the room. The grating of a metal chair against the floor made her jump. It was freezing down here, like a storage facility, which it was. She buttoned a brown wool cardigan over her black cotton cardigan, already buttoned to the clavicle. She opened her laptop, and when the gray rectangle in the upper right quadrant of the screen opened itself to prompt her

Updates Available
Do you want to restart to install these
updates now or try tonight?

she selected "Later" and then, "Remind Me Tomorrow," as she had every day for months—no, it had definitely been years. She opened the finder and clicked through the metaphorical folders until she located this week's prompt for her Writing Apocalypse course. Dorothy was an adjunct professor—a member of the "part-time" or "contingent" faculty—who taught two or three or sometimes four courses a semester in the English department and first-year writing program of a private university whose list-price tuition was twice her annual earnings. In addition to Writing Apocalypse, this semester she was also teaching Writing Affect Theory and two sections of Introduction to the Major. She had taught all the classes before and devoted to them the minimum effort required so she could write the sample chapter that would get her the contract that would get her the job that didn't exist. It didn't matter how much time she cleared; she was not making progress. All her samples had to be thrown away. She hated producing so much waste. Her subject—female confinement and the gothic novel—had become a source of nausea as her own career had come to resemble the situation of one of the characters she wrote about. She was like a poor relation who had tagged along for a weekend at a formerly grand estate and wound up marked for death by the invisible hands lurking in the wallpaper.

Last fall there had been six job openings in her field. This fall there had been none. The hiring climate had dried into a dust bowl. She couldn't go on like this, she knew, but she also couldn't not go on. She vaguely recalled a time when wanting to do the job she had trained for did not feel like too much to want. Now want itself was a thing of the past. She lived in the epilogue of wants.

She clicked around her documents, inserted a page break, and copied and pasted the grading rubric from an old assignment. Dorothy always distributed a rubric. The text was boilerplate, slightly modified from another instructor's materials. *Your paper should do more than pose a question,* it said. *It should offer at least tentative conclusions.* She hated that she had to ask the students for something she was so bad at herself. But it was easier to defend her judgments when she could point to a set of standards, an authority outside her own fancies and impressions. More than once Dorothy had ended a meeting with an unhappy student by pointing back at the rubric and shrugging helplessly before its power. She liked to imagine God musing over His spread-sheet at the end of the semester. *Locusts,* C; *Fires and Floods,* B+. *Interruptions to the Food Supply* was failing, but might do better next semester. *Plagues and Viruses* got points for participation. How *Death of the Firstborns* would do depended not only on the despair experienced by those who lost their own child but on how much panic could be stirred up in the houses of those who were skipped over. If it were up to Dorothy all courses would be pass/fail.

She did a quick Google Images search for "tsunami"—students responded better to handouts when they included pictures—and dragged to her desktop and then the Word document a computer rendering of the Statue of Liberty half-toppled in the icy New York harbor. And now, on to the reading. It was Revelation week for the students of the Apocalypse. Dorothy took from her backpack a hardcover parallel King James/New International Version Bible and flipped to the end. *And I saw a new heaven and a new earth,* the prophet wrote, *for the first heaven and the first earth were passed away; and there was no more sea.*

The sea, like death itself, would be overcome. If creation had involved dividing the land from the sea, there was a certain sense in the last chapter doing away with the sea altogether. The sea, after all, was where life began; without the sea there would be no possibility of beginning again.

Next she pulled a tattered handout from her bag: "Sinners in the Hands of an Angry God," the sermon by Jonathan Edwards, which she loved for its rich and rumbling cadences as much as for its decisive passion. *Their foot shall slide in due Time.* She assigned it hoping that the students would learn that hell was not something waiting at the *end* of life but something that could open its maw at any moment, pull you in, and devour you whole. That the threat of destruction was here and now, as was, supposedly, the reward of paradise.

At the appointed time, Edwards said, God would no longer hold them up in these slippery places.

It had been some time now since Dorothy had felt herself to be held up. She and Rog had an ongoing debate about whether the times they were living in were truly, world-historically exceptional. Rog's position had always been no, the times may be bad, but the fantasy of living in an exceptionally bad time was another version of the eschatological fantasy that one had been blessed with the great fortune of being born not somewhere in the long dull middle (muddle) of history but at its culmination, its apex, its Most Exciting Finale. These days, Dorothy was pretty sure that she actually was living at the end of something, or too many somethings to say. But as an end, it didn't have the texture of *kairos,* of, as Frank Kermode wrote, "a point in time filled with significance." It was instead the gruesome slog of *chronos,* of "passing" or "waiting" time. Ends came and came and they did not end. They sputtered and limped along. The walls of the world crept with something scabrous and bacterial, something that hovered between life and death, something that dripped and dribbled out and was flushed away. The word the doctor had used was "blighted." It sounded like something the government bailed out, a Midwestern crop failure. The dictionary on her phone said that "blight" referred to a plant disease. But Dorothy was not a plant. Of that much she was certain.

She returned to the screen and fiddled with the size of the image. Whether the statue was drowning or bobbing in the waves was impossible to say; either interpretation was a forecast of a future scenario that had evolved from unthinkable to just possible and was now likely/probable within the next ten years. "Everyone" knew this and the knowledge weighed on them and they went on acting more or less as before, which in Dorothy's mind was not evidence of stupidity or lack of care but some mixture of impotence and courage. Her therapist called it denial. "It is necessary to fully grieve for the lost future before one can build a different one," she had said the last time they talked about it. When Dorothy asked how long it took to fully grieve, her therapist shrugged in a way that seemed overdone, like she was playing to the balcony. Then: "It takes some people their whole lives," she said, in a tone so beige that Dorothy could not be sure if she meant to imply that a life of mourning was an exercise in nobility or a pathetic waste, or both, or neither.

The air was dry, and she inserted a finger into her left nostril, turning it, screwdriver-style, to release a single flake of snot. She rolled the nose shaving between her thumb and forefinger and it crumbled like plaster. Dorothy brushed it to the floor and smoothed her shoe over where she imagined it might have fallen. Her legs were itchy. She shoved a hand down her pant leg and scratched, then repeated the procedure on the other leg.

She took out her phone and checked her email: the usual junk and students asking for extensions. And this, a note from a student explaining that she would not be in class the next day because the leaderless environmental activist group of which she was a member was doing an action with a group on another campus. The student signed off with the word "together." As in, "Together, Jessie." Dorothy did not reply. She did not feel together with Jessie. She felt sympathy with Jessie's principles while also feeling that Jessie was dangerously close to exceeding the maximum allowed absences, and was going to get her grade docked by a third.

Dorothy used to love email, used to have long, meaningful, occasionally thrilling email correspondences that involved the testing of ideas and the exchange of videos and music links. Email had been the way that she and the people she knew or was getting to know had crafted personas, narrated events, made sense of their lives. That way of life, alas, had ended. Long emails had ceased being the preferred mode of storytelling among her peers, or perhaps they no longer had so much to say to one another, and emails, though sealed with perfunctory hugs and kisses, had become businesslike. Sending a thoughtful email that she had drafted over several days and edited would, she knew, be a form of aggression; it would be foisting unpaid labor, a homework assignment, on a friend. She herself liked homework, but it was unreasonable to hope for such an email: There was too much television to keep up on, and if you wanted to know what someone was doing, you could usually find out on social media. Still, Dorothy had not stopped checking, expecting, or wishing that a good message might be out there, waiting in the ether just for her.

The itch traveled down to her calves. Maybe it would help to imagine that the itch was caused by the feet of tiny angels.

The tiny angels were dancing?

The angels' feet were tiny, but were also shod in tiny pitchforks.

The angels were actually devils and they would dance on her skin until the end of time. Not in pairs, not slowly, but in an orgiastic mass, a packed club floor of ecstatic bumping and grinding, a chemical frenzy. She opened the *Times* app, squinted at the headline, closed it. A lot of people Dorothy knew said that they didn't want to have children because they couldn't count on the world existing for them. But Dorothy thought that the world simply was whatever children were born into. At least, that was the kind of thing she thought in theory. When she imagined the children of the future, the metaphorical children, they were floating on rafts roped together with the fall coats everyone had thrown away because there was no more fall, just as there was no more spring, although come brutal winter they would need to suture all the in-between-season coats together for warmth. Perhaps she should be more together with Jessie. The children of the future would ask what she had done. They would request an accounting of her preventive measures. Their laughter would be high-pitched and malnourished.

"You signed an online petition?" they would say.

"I typed my name," Dorothy clarified.

The raft children rolled their doe-like eyes. "Next you'll be telling us you composted," they said.

"No," Dorothy said, to the tops of their sweet heads. (They were looking at their phones, where some raft scandal involving parties with whom she was unacquainted was unfolding.) "I didn't like the smell."

She messed around with the scale of the box, dragging the corner to make it big, then small, then she heard a scratching and looked up. At the far end of the table a pen, attached to the hand of a youngish man with a trim beard and round, wiry glasses, was moving rapidly over the lined pages of a marble composition book. The young man or old boy was half-hidden behind a tottering pile of books, but Dorothy could see that he wore a wrinkled shirt with a collar and that his nose, which was pointed down to the page like an arrow, was conceited and very finely shaped. She couldn't see below his waist, but assumed that his boots were scuffed enough to indicate frugality and use but not so scuffed as to suggest rough use or poverty. He stopped writing for a moment to rub his forehead, and Dorothy saw, to her amazement, that the elbows of his jacket were patched. He looked like a stock image of a young professor, which suggested he was, in fact, an advanced graduate student, someone engaged in the time-honored pursuit of faking it till making it. At the summit of his pile was the familiar Hackett edition of Kant's Third Critique, a tome that managed to appear imposing while still calling to mind the color of berry nail polish. It was by far the thickest book on the pile and ought to have been placed at the bottom to ensure the stability of the tower, but the student had either an imminent need to consult it or a desire that it be seen, or perhaps he found its presence inspiring in some way, like just having in plain view its greatness (as personified by its cover) goaded him osmotically to his own higher greatness. Dorothy strained to make out the titles of the other books, but she couldn't read the spines and didn't recognize the colors or typographies. The student must have felt Dorothy's eyes because he looked up and before Dorothy could look away their eyes met and where Dorothy expected to see coolness or contempt, or perhaps a hint of sexual interest/flirtation or at least curiosity/assessment/rejection, she saw only a blankness; the student stared right through her, his mouth a little slack, so soft and unguarded it was obscene, and all the while his hand continued to move across the page. Then, with a decisive vigor, he shook his pen—it was a fountain pen—and returned his disinterested but committed gaze to the unblank page. He gripped it like a chisel and bore down on the tip with all his meager weight.

It was the shake of the pen, efficient and practiced, that made Dorothy begin to suspect that the student was slightly performing his role, relishing the appearance of intellectual labor, aware, more than she had originally surmised, of having an audience. At some earlier times of life Dorothy might have assumed that the show was somehow tailored to her, that it meant something about how he as an individual felt about her as an individual—whatever individuality he could conjure from her books, her clothing, appearance, expression, etc.—but by now she had come to understand that most social interactions were matters of function and role. She was there but she was not there. Like the love of one's parents, or being someone's type, or being born into the generation destined to witness the end of the world, it wasn't personal.

The Kantian, if that's what he was, again bent over his

notebook, with his head slightly turned toward the wall. His hair was very short, it had been trimmed with an electric razor, and Dorothy could see an angry red pimple on his otherwise soft, ghost-white neck. She felt a rush of inexpressible tenderness, a longing to cradle him and kiss the spot where the razor or perhaps the toxins in the environment or perhaps his own genetic propensity to blemishes had oiled and irritated the skin. At one time Dorothy would have been curious to know what he was writing, would have wanted to soak up secondhand his painstakingly constructed argument, but now, faced with his raw youth, concentrated in the red spot on his neck, her only impulse was to scream: *Save yourself! Before it's too late!* With sadness she turned back to her screen, which had gone dark. Out of the corner of her eye she watched as the student raised his gaze to the ceiling and tapped his chin with the pen. A ridiculous gesture.

She jabbed the space bar to wake up her computer and saved her document to the cloud. Did her comrade of the stacks feel joy as his pen moved over the page? Did he bask in the oceanic feeling of his mind expanding as it synthesized and surpassed the wisdom of the ages? He seemed to be filling the notebook faster now, turning the pages hurriedly as the pen scratched and flew, as if compelled by some angel of his own to get down the words before they ran away. Dorothy comforted herself with the thought that his flow of writing would have to stop, that even if his thoughts continued unimpeded he would run out of room in the notebook, and she was just losing interest in the whole pantomime of success when the student raked back his chair, threw his books in a twill duffel bag, and departed, as if he had suddenly remembered an appointment for which he was terribly late. He trotted away lightly, but his right shoulder was pulled down so far by the weight of the bag that he reminded Dorothy of a broken marionette, and the figure he cut under the harsh yellow lights was solitary and doomed. Without him the stacks were creepy and deserted, and she missed his company.

An hour later she ascended from the bowels of the library. It was raining heavily, and with one wet hand she held down the broken rib of her umbrella, lest her fellow pedestrians be impaled on the cheapness of her consumer goods. She tried to visualize the mountain of things such as umbrellas she had thrown away in her lifetime and multiplied that by three hundred million people in America alone, catching a vertiginous glimpse of the garbage sublime. It was as advertised: a feeling of passion and terror.

She was half a block from the subway when the rain suddenly ceased. She stopped to shake out her umbrella and the canvassers emerged from the mist like rainbows, shedding their plastic ponchos and taking the first steps of their eager sidewalk tangos, one skinny in round wire glasses with a toothbrush moustache and the other pink and bearish with a belly that he pushed forward when he walked, like it meant that he could be trusted.

"Do you have a minute for the environment?" the moustache asked. His tone was a master class of contradictions whose overriding effect was to signal that he was aware of the absurdity of his performance and was, like Dorothy, just trying to make it day by day in America. Unlike waiters, who never dropped their masks, the best canvassers foregrounded the awkwardness of the situation to create a temporary bond of fellowship that dared you to defy their good humor.

"I already donate," Dorothy lied.

"Thank you!" Moustache enthused, holding his palm out for a high-five. "Have a rocking day."

She looked up at the sky, as if something very interesting were up there—and then it was! Up in the clear yonder, where the clouds had vanished so quickly they seemed to be guiltily fleeing the scene of a crime, was—a rainbow! An actual ROY G BIV of celestial wavelengths! God had seen her lie and declared it Good! He parted the heavens and smiled His favor upon her!

Instead of slapping Moustache's hand forcefully, and thus producing the distinctive clap of a successful high-five, Dorothy's hand limply tangled with his. All of their fingers were damp.

"It's cool, it's cool," he assured her, snapping and hitting his fists together in a fluttering jig. "Next time!"

Dorothy wiped her hand on her pants to rid herself of the interaction. She was at once mortified and stupefied at how easy it had been, and as she descended the stairs she looked back, fearing and a little hoping that Moustache would have realized his error, and followed her underground to collect what she owed.

Down on the subway tracks two rats were fighting for an empty fun-size chip bag. The victor ran away with the bag between his teeth to lick the crumbs of salt in private. The raft children would mock her mercilessly for what she had done with the canvassers. Worse, they would mock her for feeling bad about it. "Nobody cares about your ten dollars a month," they would say as the sunlight broke through the tattered sails, dappling the weathered logs of the decks. "You should have chained yourself to a power plant."

There was no land in sight, so she had time to justify herself while they sailed along—the rafts had sails, they were sail rafts. "I found it draining to live zagging and zigging from exhaustion to emergency and back again," she said. "I craved the simple privacy of not being a political actor." The rats came back into view. Maybe they were different rats. By their smirks it was clear that the children did not accept the possibility of an apolitical life. "I had to buttress the borders of my self," Dorothy said, "which was regularly assaulted to the point of porousness by digital media." By their grins it was clear that they had long ago given up on wholeness. The seas, which had been calm, were starting to get agitated, and the children were losing interest in her. The waves rose up and the older ones tied the little ones to the masts for safety. "I hate group work," Dorothy tried. "My personality is all wrong for cooperative action. For action in general." Those who were not too busy securing the sails twisted their mouths with scorn in her direction, making clear that they who navigated the choppy seas because Dorothy had been too burdened by her bad personality to overthrow the government were not in the business of forgiving and exonerating. "Whatever I did," Dorothy concluded lamely, "I regretted it." The children had no patience for self-pity. They pointed to their raft and answered in chorus, "We live on a raft. Our exhaustion does not toggle with emergency. We live one hundred percent in an emergent state."

"But you haven't known anything else," Dorothy said to the raft children. One little girl's hair had flown into her face, but because her hands were tied to the mast she could only furiously toss her head to try to whip the hair back; Dorothy wanted to help her but knew her touch would be unwelcome. "Whereas I was raised to expect a future. Everyone said that to increase my standard of living, all I had to do was follow my dreams."

"No one said that," the little girl said from behind her salt-crusted hair.

"What is a dream?" asked the other raft children. "What is the future?"

They rowed closer to shore—and now Dorothy was on her own raft, which for some reason had a mermaid on its prow, which doubled as a charging station. She plugged her phone into the mermaid and checked her email. Junk. Receipts.

Fundraising appeals. Even in her apocalyptic fantasies, no one ever emailed her. The age of email was over.

The train arrived, crammed. She stood, then sat at the first opening. A fat woman in a puffy coat squeezed next to her. At first Dorothy stiffened to make room, then found herself mindlessly relaxing against the coat's shoulder, sinking into it until she encountered the meaty resistance of arm beneath pillow. The woman in the puffer elbowed her gently but firmly away. Even if some coat-to-coat contact was unavoidable in the subway crush, it was still bad manners to touch strangers. Dorothy, conceding her error, but unable to take up any less space, stood again and leaned her shoulder against the pole. She took from her bag the Kafka story she had started reading on the train into Manhattan that morning. Dorothy always read on the subway. It was the best way to absent yourself from your surroundings. The human sublime was worse than the garbage sublime. It would kill you to confront the agonies and joys pressed together in the crowd, in one single subway car. Each person with their disappointments, their millstones, their pleasures, their loves. Each person living a life only they could live. The only recourse was to hide somehow, to deaden oneself to the cacophony of pulsing, repulsive existence.

The story was narrated by a dog. Where Dorothy picked it up, the dog was explaining dog-nature, its desire for intimacy and the strictures put upon it. *We are impelled to be together,* the dog said, *and nothing can prevent us from satisfying that urge; all our laws and institutions, the few I still know, and the numberless ones I have forgotten, they all go back to the greatest happiness that exists for us, our warm companionableness. And now the obverse.* Dorothy looked down at the woman in the puffer, who had closed her eyes. Her head was lolling back against the wall beneath a poem about roast chicken that the

Metropolitan Transit Authority hung in the subways as a public service. The woman was older than it had first seemed; her skin was wrinkled as a walnut shell. Dorothy returned to her book.

All this poor dog wanted was to be near other dogs, to greet them and sniff between their legs, and yet for obscure or ungiven reasons there was a prohibition against it. An event of some kind had separated the dogs from one another. *We, who want to be together . . . we of all creatures live remote from one another, in curious callings, which are often hard for the dog next door to understand . . .*

Maybe it wasn't an event. Maybe it was just history. At some times some things kept the dogs together and at other times other things tore them apart. Or maybe the separation had to do with temperament. The narrator-dog was one of those who asks too many questions, who focuses on the negative, who allows himself to be irritated by what doesn't quite fit. *Withdrawn, solitary, entirely taken up with my small, hopeless—but to me—indispensable inquiries . . .* This dog had to stand apart. But he was too porous, that was his problem; he let everything in. That was why the musical dogs, the pack whose every step was singing, had such power over him. They annihilated him with their music, forcing him into sensations that did not, strictly speaking, belong to him. Feelings, Dorothy often tried to explain to her students, could be catching as a cold. You never knew ahead of time how sick they could make you.

The shoes were in a heap, the unread magazines were piled on the table, the dust was visible on multiple surfaces, and no one had done last night's dishes. Several minutes of life that Dorothy would never get back were passed swirling a piece of toilet paper over the bathroom floor to gather and discard the strands of hair she had missed that morning. Holding open the refrigerator door, she took a long drink of seltzer directly from the bottle, closed the refrigerator, and checked her email. Nothing. Waiting time was agony, particularly when one had no idea what one was waiting *for*.

She got up from the couch, walked ten feet, and threw herself onto the bed. She looked at the window and saw reflected against the dark background an indistinct human shape. She opened the bank application on her phone and checked the balance. Scrolling through the account, she felt the usual rising tide of panic accompanied by the also-usual numb sense that her decisions were bad because they could not matter; as she would never get ahead, there was no reason not to fall behind. She got out of the bed and tugged shut the gray curtain, wiping her own face from the windowpane. On her way out of the room she caught sight of her midsection in the mirror that rested against the wall between the bed and the dresser. The ancient notion that art holds up a mirror to reality was complicated in the eighteenth century by the idea that the mirror of art ought to reflect only certain parts of reality, those that people should imitate. Then there was Oscar Wilde: *It is the spectator, and not life, that art really mirrors.*

"Okay!" said Dorothy out loud, stressing the exclamation. She retrieved the toolbox from under the kitchen sink and located nails and hammer. A change would do her good. She hung the mirror on the wall, horizontal-wise. She stepped back and noted with satisfaction that she could no longer see below her neck.

Back on the couch with the bottle of seltzer. The couch creaking gently, like a boat at sea. Dorothy thought about the bleached-white coral. She thought about the icebergs and microplastics. The raft children were floating back into view when it happened, the turn of the key and Rog was in the room. He peeled her a clementine. One by one she curled off the white veins and collected them in her hand. The juice rinsed her teeth.

"Hey," Rog said, coming out of the bedroom in an old T-shirt, now stretched tight across the middle. "Did you hang the mirror sideways?"

The foot pedal of the trash can was broken, so Dorothy pried up the lid with a finger and flapped her other hand over the bag until the pith floated down. Pondering lace, snow, feather pillows, and other softnesses she hadn't seen in years. Tallying, for the umpteenth time, the kitchen trash times a billion. The landfills would be ancient ruins that the giant cockroaches of the future would revel in as palaces. She and Rog really did need to start composting. What they would do with all that fertile soil, Dorothy had no idea. Leave it downstairs on the free table in the lobby? Would their neighbors know what to do?

"Why," she said, "do people always ask if you've done something instead of asking why you did it?"

"There are no 'people' here," Rog said, too sweetly, like he was speaking for the record and wanted to be found blameless. "It's just me. The actual person you live with."

The rage flared so suddenly that Dorothy closed her eyes to block it out. She exhaled and counted down like her therapist had taught her. The feeling passed.

"Anyway," said Rog, "now I'm just a head. I can't see if my clothes match."

Dorothy shrugged. Like many of their interactions since the onset of the blight, this one was at once fraught and deflated. Dorothy was neither disappointed in Rog nor gratified by him. She had entered a period in which he did not pertain.

She riffled through the stack of mail, and while Rog put spaghetti on plates she retrieved her phone from the rug and checked the bank balance again. They ate the spaghetti on the bed while watching a cartoon about a depressed horse. Dorothy liked the show's theme song, which played over the end credits, but the Web-based streaming service automatically started the next episode before the song ended, so while Rog looked at his phone she paused the second episode, navigated back to the menu, selected the episode they had just concluded, fast-forwarded through it until the credits, and quickly double-clicked to prevent the next episode from playing. It was perverse, the effort a person had to exert to achieve closure.

"You know how we used to joke about how we wanted to be the first to die in the apocalypse?" Dorothy said, when the brief and poignant song had faded. "Because our glasses would break?"

"Do we have to talk about this now?" Rog asked, standing up with his dirty plate in hand.

She rubbed the tops of her feet, which ached from causes she could not identify, and followed him into the kitchen. While in the past, she said, it would have made sense to die in the first wave—to burn up in a nuclear holocaust, for example—in the present, ongoing, mobile disaster one should aspire to survive, hide, and migrate. To be the tiny rodent darting among the corpses of dinosaurs. To be the rat with the fun-size chip bag.

Rog's head was in the refrigerator. "Did you do any work today?" he asked.

"This is what my class is *about*," said Dorothy. "There won't be one sudden and final end everywhere but many small ends in different places. The world is ending all the time but only in a limited and immediate radius. It's not the nuclear fear we were raised on."

"Who is this 'we' you're referring to?" asked Rog. "What decade were you born in?"

Rog cracked a beer and winced at the sound. Dorothy ignored him. Rog was a minimizer, and while minimizers had their usefulness re: tamping down mass hysteria, it was important not to be derailed by them. What a strange and old-fashioned collective experience, she said, the idea that people could all die together in one heaven-bound moment; today you had to first watch other people, some of whom lived very far away and others of whom were technically neighbors, die online, and you couldn't save them, and all the while you could be next. It almost made you understand the appeal of a cult. And although it was redundant to wish for your own death at the first sign of trouble, she went on, pulling a piece of semi-hard spaghetti up from the bottom of the unwashed pot and chewing it contemplatively, although one had to seek habitable ground, one could not let geographic strategy blind oneself to the overwhelming power and machinations of fortune. Resigning oneself to fate was the key.

The spaghetti was chewy and also crunchy. She pried up another piece (only a little starch got lodged in her fingernail) and ate that one, too. Water was running in the sink while Rog told the dishwasher, with a little smile, that he was glad Dorothy no longer intended to kill herself as soon as she ran out of contact lenses, which for years had been her solution, back when worst-case survival scenarios were the subject of a popular board game.

"Do you ever think about being dragged for miles in a mud-slide?" Dorothy asked the empty Tupperware container Rog had taken out of the cupboard to store the extra sauce, making no move to put sauce into it.

"The people who die in natural disasters are the people who don't heed the warnings to get out," Rog said, not unkindly.

"I'm asking what it feels like," said Dorothy. "Not who deserves it.

"What about the people who get burned alive in their cars driving from the fires?" Dorothy pressed on. "The fires start so fast, they don't have time to be warned."

Rog's idea of comfort was to say the same thing over and over until Dorothy capitulated to reason. "We don't live in a fire zone," he said. "And if we are ever warned to evacuate, we will evacuate right away."

"Trust me," Dorothy said. "I would be only too happy to be forced to abandon everything."

Rog shot her a wounded look. "Thanks," he said.

"Not you," she said. "I just mean, imagine if you came home one day and the apartment had burned to the ground. Imagine how free you would feel."

"If you want to declutter," said Rog, "that's a different conversation."

Dorothy reached down and rearranged the plates in the dishwasher to maximize the space. In the drying rack the knives were sticking blade up at attention. She asked which glass was hers and Rog couldn't remember so she dumped both and took a new one from the cupboard and filled it with water from the sink and drank it. She retrieved her phone from the couch. The rainbow was all over Instagram. She liked photos until she ran out of photos to like. She raked her fingers through her hair and spun the strands into a little clump that she thrust into her pocket to deal with later.

"When's the last time you disinfected your phone?" she yelled to the kitchen, but he was saying something about the rainbow.

Rog sat down on the couch and looked at his phone. Dorothy sat next to him and looked at her phone.

"Hey," Rog said, glancing up. "Did you have therapy today?"

Dorothy shook her head. "I canceled it," she said.

"But she's the cheap one," he said, and, when Dorothy didn't laugh, asked in his serious tone, which was lower and more deliberate, if she was okay. Dorothy shrugged.

"It's none of her business," she said.

A good thing about Rog was that he knew how to respect

someone's privacy. He believed in the ideal of *protecting the solitude of the other*. He didn't say, "You pay her to make things her business," or, "You can talk about it with me," or even, "It was mine, too." He had a tact that was rare, or maybe he had other things to do. He kissed the top of Dorothy's head and went into the bedroom. Dorothy stayed on the couch and took out the Kafka story. She had to finish it; she had to finish something. As she read she took notes to make sure she was paying attention. The little dog wanted answers but could not get them. Something unspeakable forbade the singing dogs from making contact, even though greetings seemed to be fundamental to dog law. And why did they keep standing up and showing their genitals? Why were they so compelled to expose their shame? Was it an act of aggression or abjection? *They bared themselves, and exposed their nakedness to full view* and in so doing had been expelled from the community, lost their status as dogs, which would explain—

Suddenly a crash.

"Fuck!" Rog exclaimed.

He had been taking the mirror down when it slipped and banged on the floor and cracked. There wasn't any broken glass to be swept away but now whichever way you hung it, it split you in two—like a magician had come along, dazzled the crowd with half a trick, and forgotten to put you back together.

"I'll order a new one," said Dorothy.

She put the story aside and opened the browser on her phone. She found the same mirror or one close enough and bought it; she checked her email for the confirmation and marked it as read. Productivity begat productivity. She plumped the pillows on the sofa and put away Rog's shoes that were littered across the rooms. She got a paper bag out from under the sink and collected all the credit card offers, magazines, catalogs, and notices from congressional representatives that were spread across two tables and a credenza.

She threw away their bank statement, first ripping it into tiny strips to protect their personal information. She swiped under the sofa with a paper towel to collect the stray hairs and dust. She straightened the piles of books and hung Rog's jackets and belts that were draped over the furniture and after that she felt much better.

It was too late to think any more. Dorothy changed her panty liner (she wore the kind with wings) and rinsed out her nightguard, which no matter how much warm water she ran it under, remained a yellowish shade of tartar and permanently speckled with black. She clicked it over her teeth (it trapped saliva onto a coat over the teeth, which seemed to counteract re: hygiene whatever benefits it conferred re: grinding) and swallowed. She got under the covers, curling herself into a ball so tight that Rog would not dare touch her anywhere but on her head. He put her to bed, petting her like a cat, saying, "Sweet dreams" and "shhhhh." Four hours later she woke fully rested from a successful REM cycle, sat at the table, and finished "Investigations of a Dog." She didn't understand why the dog ended the story by talking about freedom. *What,* she thought, *does freedom have to do with anything?* She had never been liberated by investigation. *How sad*, she thought, *to be jealous of a fictional dog.* She went back to bed, wearing earplugs this time, to block out the snuffling noises that emanated from Rog's mouth. An hour later, when she woke up to pee, she popped out the nightguard and left it, sticky with saliva, on the dresser that doubled as a nightstand.

Her eyes were slow to adjust to the harsh bathroom light. When she wiped, something stringy was on the paper and she felt it snap back a little, so she put a finger inside and pulled. A short elastic band of gunk came out, looped around the first knuckle. She rubbed her fingers together and deposited it in the toilet, where it settled on the surface of the water like kelp. The blood on the panty liner was jewel red and gelatinous and a little thinner and underneath it was brown like dead leaves. She rubbed a finger on the red part and put the finger on her tongue.

She had never tasted menstrual blood, but she had to assume it was the same taste, although it was possible, of course, that pregnancy hormones had saturated the blood and affected the taste. Maybe she was tasting hormones, or stale hormones. Dorothy didn't know enough to know if that was scientific or not, and anyway she couldn't think of anything to compare the taste to. Without a comparison she had no way to understand what was happening and no way to remember it. She wouldn't be able to tell anyone about it.

She wiped again, trying to get more on her finger, and tasted it again. If she had been served the glop as a pâté on bread at a fancy restaurant she could have been convinced, without a lot of effort, that it was a delicacy, and she would probably have eaten the whole thing and not been revolted, even if she was only eating it because it had been served to her and because she was going to pay for it. But the blood, if that was even what it was, was so viscous that her tongue didn't seem able to absorb it properly; it rolled on the surface and lingered, strangely, in the back of her throat. Was it lining? Was it tissue? And what was tissue made of, anyway? Was there something to it, or was it tissue all the way down?

She flushed. She rolled the panty liner into a tiny ball and wrapped the ball neatly in toilet paper and buried it in the trash under her hair. She drank handfuls of tap water from the bathroom sink but the taste was still there, in the back of her throat, metallic, keeping her awake for some time.

THE NEXT DAY

Dorothy was still in bed the next morning when her phone vibrated. Her best friend, Gaby.

Gaby: Yooooooo

It was an ongoing feature of Dorothy and Gaby's textual communication that repeated letters or punctuation marks were used to signal enthusiasm and intimacy. In the absence of these orthographic quirks, which constituted a kind of adolescent drag, both felt insecure, and with good cause: In their well-educated hands, proper spelling could be a cold formality; a properly placed period, a knife.

Dorothy: hiiiiii
Gaby: We've been partying since FIVE

The words appeared in a box against Dorothy's lock screen, a screenshot of a Pierre Bonnard painting called *Young Woman Writing*. It showed a woman scribbling over a red tablecloth, with squares of white paper all around. Dorothy liked that the woman was intently focused, or perhaps collapsing, heapishly, over something that the viewer would never be able to read. She had heard it suggested that the papers were some work of art or letters to a great love. She liked to imagine the woman was writing her grocery list, or doing her taxes.

She pressed on the message and entered Rog's birth date to unlock her phone, and a photo popped into the chat: Gaby's baby, Sherman, in a Black Flag onesie and suede slippers. Sherman had a hawkish nose and a round face smushed into a cube of skull. The effect was that of a cute and old-fashioned bowl placed on a square plate. This morning his flat black hair was sticking in every direction like a punkish halo, and he was looking coyly to the side. Before her best friend had a baby Dorothy had not known that babies were flirts.

Dorothy: Aw!!!!!!!!!!!!!

Gaby took this as an invitation to send another photo. Dorothy's fondness for Sherman was mostly theoretical—she was not one of those women who love babies qua babies and fantasize, for example, about eating them—but she did enjoy the photos, if only as a way to stay in touch with her friend. In this one, Sherman's eyes were squeezed shut and his mouth was gaped wide. He was crying. Dorothy could see that there was an underlying comedy to all despair that was specially revealed in an exaggerated infantile expression, but she couldn't help mentally criticizing Gaby for delaying the giving of comfort in order to snap a photo. But maybe Sherman hadn't been crying when she first held up the phone? Maybe he started crying *because* she held up the phone? It seemed unethical to take a photo of a crying child, but Dorothy couldn't say why. Equally in the case of crying or smiling, the photographer distanced herself, electing to document rather than participate in the child's feeling. That it seemed worse to do that with sorrow than with joy suggested that culturally, joy had been given short shrift.

Gaby was not being cruel or unfeeling by sending Dorothy these early-morning baby pictures. Dorothy hadn't told her about the pregnancy, and anyway, she didn't mind the photos.

This flesh and blood creature with hair and teeth who wore slippers made from animal hide and who labored tirelessly to perfect the art of transferring objects from one hand to the other had no connection that she could see to her situation. Gaby would have agreed, if Dorothy had told her, which she would have, much as she would have told her therapist, except when she was about to, Gaby had started talking about her birthday, which had recently passed. They had been sitting on the sectional in Gaby's apartment, facing each other, socked toes nearly touching. Gaby was trying to explain the relief of aging out of people's misperceptions of her. She had crossed the Rubicon, she said.

"Like Caesar," Dorothy had joked.

Gaby's eyes were runny, two undercooked eggs. She did not like the reference. "No," she said, pulling away her feet and tucking them underneath her. "I'm not an emperor."

"I know," said Dorothy. "I just meant that Caesar also—"

"I don't think I'm Julius fucking Caesar," Gaby said.

"I'm sorry," Dorothy said. "I don't think that you're an emperor, or that you think that you're an emperor, or whatever."

Gaby pushed her glasses to the top of her head and rubbed tears from her eyes. This quality of tenderness was new in Gaby, and Dorothy assumed it was hormonal. The glasses were extra-large gold-wire aviators that had been purchased at the pharmacy on one of those plastic racks that spin. Whether or not they were fake was a matter of debate between Dorothy and Rog; it really depended on what you meant by fake. Technically there was a magnification of vision involved, although it was so small as to seem an insult to the truly vision-impaired. But the bigger issue was that Gaby was the kind of person who could make wearing glasses from the pharmacy seem chic. She had that inborn and absolute style that money can only partly explain and motherhood had not diminished.

She pulled the frames back down over her face and explained that what she meant about the Rubicon was that she had crossed to the place where no one expected anything of her. She had tried various careers (law school, journalism, play-writing, documentary film-making) but had failed to fulfill her youthful promise—not because she was an interesting lost cause, but because the promise itself had been overstated. On this birthday in particular, her first since having Sherman, she had felt keenly and unmistakably that the world had given up on her. But it wasn't a failure. It was a becoming.

"Everyone thought I was precocious," Gaby said, "but that was never true. I was just young."

Dorothy, who had known Gaby for ten years, thought that Gaby *had* been precocious, but she had also been indecisive and easily bored, and unwilling to work hard and improve incrementally. But what Gaby said helped Dorothy clarify something she had been struggling for some time to put into words.

"I feel the same way," Dorothy said. "It's like every time I don't get a job, my own sense of fraudulence gets closer to being accepted as the truth I always knew it was."

"I have a job," said Gaby, who was spending ten hours a week fact-checking a book on the history of surveillance written by a friend of her father's, and who had not entirely forgiven Dorothy for the Julius Caesar moment. "I mean, you have a job, too."

"We both have jobs," said Dorothy, aware that this was the kind of thing most people didn't have to insist on.

"You should have a baby," Gaby said. "I can't tell you what a relief it is to be needed. Sherman would *die* without me. It's good for my self-esteem."

Dorothy, who at that point had not decided one way or another what should be kept and what thrown away, said only, "I know."

He looked betrayed. His eyes, shocked with a new awareness of pain. His arms, reaching up, out, to be held.

Dorothy: poor Shermie—is he OK?!
Gaby: Yah he's fine . . . I keep meaning to tell you I met someone who is writing a book about Daphne du Maurier
Dorothy: !!!!!!

Years ago, Dorothy had the ambition to write a popular biography of Daphne du Maurier, the author of her favorite novel, *Rebecca*. At that time Dorothy was fresh off her first publication, an article about du Maurier and Carolina Nabuco, who claimed that du Maurier plagiarized her novel *A Sucessora*. It was an early triumph that Dorothy would fail to surpass or even match. While riding high on this success— which in the years since had come to seem small, and therefore humiliating, especially in light of its accompanying feeling of achievement, of having "made it"—Dorothy fantasized that she might enjoy a notable career, that she could be a scholar who taught at a top-tier research university and wrote books for the general reader that would be reviewed in the daily paper. She had long since abandoned such ambitions, and remembering them made her shrink from herself in agony, but Gaby, even as she changed careers in the enthusiastic, slightly idiotic way that some people fall in love, believing each new affair will last, had held Dorothy to this ideal. Gaby had a lot invested in the notion that Dorothy could do what she had set out to do. Gaby had no way of understanding what a decade in academia could do to a person, but if she had, Dorothy wouldn't have wanted to be friends with her.

Dorothy: is OK it's an honor just to be a superfan
Gaby: She seems dumb anyway
Gaby: This woman I met, not DDM

Dorothy: Right right
Dorothy: What else
Dorothy: Heyyyyy?

Gaby was busy, or she had lost interest, or she had suffered a stroke and Sherman was crying with outstretched arms and there was no one in the room to feed him or take his picture or prevent him rolling off the bed into an accident Dorothy tried not to picture, but it was too late, she saw it, the crushed skull, the still body. Dorothy sent an emoji with hearts for eyes and thumbed over the headlines. She rolled to the edge of the bed and tugged on the curtain. The sky was a thick impasto of white. It looked freshly poured and wet, as if you could leave footprints in it. She pulled down her underwear to see if there was any new blood. There wasn't. Gravity had yet to do its morning work.

She didn't regret not telling Gaby, but it made her feel far away, like she was drifting in the ocean and Gaby was back on shore. If only there was some way to have the intimacy of telling without losing control over the story. That was the worst, when all your little pieces got scattered around. Rog got up and they drank coffee while looking at their phones. After he left, she took a shower and put on pants and looked at the article by Silvan Tomkins she was teaching later that day and then it was time to go into the city for a session with her second therapist.

Rog insisted, whenever Dorothy asked for reassurance, which was often, that he didn't mind that she was spending money they could have been saving for an apartment or retirement on therapy. "First of all," he would say, "would we really be saving it? I think we would just waste it on takeout and frivolities." This word, "frivolities," was characteristic of Rog, who had the questionable gift of turning his and Dorothy's worst qualities into a joke. Some people, he added, his voice hinting at an obscure knowledge of human vice, had far worse and more expensive habits. Dorothy went as far as to offer to pay for the second therapist out of her own paycheck, but that would have required an overhaul of their entire fiscal scenario. Rog always said that it was merely an accident of history that his labor, which involved project management and a software company, was compensated at a rate higher than Dorothy's, and as this recompense had no inherent relationship to their respective human worth—a word that betrayed the deep cultural bias toward the economic—it made no sense *not* to redistribute his salary, which could hardly go by the name "wealth," and was anyway not so great by New York standards, though it dwarfed Dorothy's—the point was that their finances were all mixed together, "joint," making them by some measures more married than their married friends who maintained separate accounts. But on this point Rog would not negotiate. He did not want to be in a relationship where pennies were counted and receipts were submitted. Neither did Dorothy.

Dorothy's second therapist had the inside office of a suite on the seventh floor of a building downtown. Her waiting room doubled as a real estate agent's office. The broker was a smoother operator than the slobs and hustlers from whom Dorothy had rented apartments. He wore slim-fitting suits that hit at the ankle, and smelled like a hair salon. Once Dorothy had trailed him from the subway to the office, the length of an entire block. There had been some activists blocking the sidewalk that day, protesting the bank next door for funding a tar sands operation. "Get a job," the broker yelled as he shoved his way through the picket. Dorothy could have predicted the broker's contempt, but the nakedness of his hatred, how he didn't feel he had to hide it—that was surprising.

Today he sat at the desk with his earbuds in, breathing noisily, listening to what seemed to be a guided meditation. On the table in front of Dorothy was a tattered copy of *Psychology Today*. YOUR DEEPEST SECRETS: WHAT YOU HIDE, EVEN FROM YOURSELF. The watercooler burped. Dorothy pulled out her phone. On Twitter, Alexandra was sharing some personal news.

Alexandra was a former member of Dorothy's cohort who was on the tenure track at Northwestern. "Friends (and enemies, ha), my book has been acquired by Oxford!" she had tweeted. Dorothy scanned the replies. She knew or recognized most of the names chiming in—young professors scattered around the good schools on either coast, a few ambitious grad students who had learned to leverage the power of social media, and Dorothy's and Alexandra's former adviser, Judith Robinson. Most everyone confined themselves to "congratulations" or the champagne emoji; a couple asked what the book was about. Judith had replied, "I expect nothing less."

It had been some time since Dorothy had felt herself to be in Judith's favor, but to witness Alexandra publicly claimed in this way was nonetheless gutting. Dorothy exhaled so loudly that the broker opened his eyes to glare at her. "Sorry," she said, and regretted saying it. He closed his eyes and his first fingers and thumbs floated toward one another as if of their own accord.

Dissertation advisers, like parents, have favorites. For the first three or four years of grad school Dorothy had assumed that she was Judith's favorite, because Judith trusted her with so many tasks, from alphabetizing books to footnoting articles and even house sitting. She made Dorothy privy to departmental gossip, and once had set Dorothy up with a professor from another school. (It didn't work out; the professor's divorce was not as final as Judith had led Dorothy to believe.) Dorothy had assumed that Judith's attention was a sign of interest in her work. But one day in office hours Dorothy happened to overhear, while waiting outside the cracked door (the excuse for leaving the door cracked was always Judith's demand for fresh air, but it was widely acknowledged that Judith believed that whatever she said to one person was worth hearing by the entire department), her beloved adviser, a titan, a woman who broke major ground, exclaim that the argument Alexandra was working out in her article draft was "significant."

"Significant" was not a word that anyone had ever used in relation to Dorothy's writing. She heard "clever" or "bright" or "promising," a word that contains in it the threat of being broken. Even when she published her du Maurier article, no one had believed it to be "paradigm-shifting" or "field-defining," which everyone knew were the aims of twenty-first-century literary scholarship. It was, instead, "very good," and "relevant," and even, one of the readers said—and Dorothy still wasn't sure whether this was meant as a compliment—"stylish." Not "significant."

While Alexandra was basking in her anointment, thrumming with pride, Dorothy was pretending to be too engrossed in a passage from Pierre Bourdieu's *Distinction* to be eavesdropping—though again, it could hardly be called eavesdropping when they had wanted her to hear everything. She held the book, which was enormously large and heavy, high up to her face, hoping to indicate fascination and ease—that while she was too engrossed in Bourdieu's important text to notice whoever was exiting the office, she did not *have* to be engrossed; she was not confused or struggling. On the contrary, her interest had the lightness and breeziness of a person enjoying a wonderful conversation with a dear old friend who happens to be the most popular kid in school. She was absorbed but effortlessly; she just really liked it! Usually Dorothy underlined her books with a heavy hand and filled the margins with bewildered asterisks and question marks, indicating passages to which she must return in order to obtain even a shred of comprehension, but that day she forced her hand to flippantly issue little check marks, bubbly evidence of offhand agreement, of her capacity to quickly scan a text and intuit its most important points, which were so transparent that they hardly needed annotating, except that it was a habit—habit, *habitus,* ha!; or maybe it appeared that she had read this book so many times already that these check marks were ultracasual greetings or reminders, just a cursory dip back into extremely familiar territory. Check! As she waited for Alexandra to leave Judith's office, Dorothy's hand issued check after happy check—check!—conscious as she did that she was producing a chaos of checks, a senseless chorus of dim-witted marginal accord. Then Alexandra tapped her on the shoulder and Dorothy jumped, sending a line of graphite across one of Bourdieu's famous charts and dragging the point of the mechanical pencil through the page.

"Oops," Alexandra said. "You tore it."

She peered down. "Wow, you really like this page," she added.

Dorothy smiled without teeth and shoved the book into her bag.

"She's ready for you," Alexandra said.

Judith, her yellow hair folded atop her head like a crown or a rope of bread, her mouth slashed with her signature cakey red lipstick, waved a hand to invite Dorothy in. As Dorothy rose, Alexandra made a show of holding the door, which was already open. Dorothy interpreted this action of door-holding, which a stranger would have described, if they noticed it at all, as desultory politeness, as Alexandra's way of drawing attention to the door itself, i.e., to herself, i.e., to Alexandra, because Alexandra's research was about doors. Specifically, the function of doors in the Victorian novel. In actuality, Alexandra probably held the door in order to remain a few extra seconds in Judith's vicinity, to absorb the full glory of her anointing, or perhaps the courtesy of holding the door was an unconscious apology, an attempt to make up for having received Judith's blessing, which Alexandra would have understood without being told was an act of aggression against Dorothy. But at the time Dorothy had felt that Alexandra, rather than holding back the door, was in fact pointing to it, forcing Dorothy to reckon with its power. *Behold, scholarship! Cross ye the threshold of marketable, field-defining monographs!*

Since she had first known Alexandra to be a student (soon-to-be teacher) of doors, Dorothy had assumed that she had some theory about the meaning of doors. But a few weeks after the *Distinction* incident, at a colloquium where Alexandra was presenting the same article Judith had been praising, Dorothy realized that Alexandra was really interested in—doors. Who made them. Out of what kind of wood. Popular designs; the door vs. the folding screen. And so forth.

There had been unusually high attendance at that meeting, either because Alexandra was a rising star in the department or because people wanted to impress Judith with their attendance; Dorothy still recalled Judith nodding and smiling serenely as Alexandra expounded on the subject of—doors. Not what they were *about*—just that they were. The fact of them. Their bare existence. Whether or not a doorknob was mentioned in relation to the door. Whether a door was pushed or pulled open. Which authors mentioned doors and which took the existence of doors for granted, passing over them in silence, and thus revealing something deeper and more nefarious than those who took the trouble to include them in the inventory of a room. What, Alexandra asked her fellow students in a teacherly tone, are the *politics* of doors? What *power relations* do they indicate?

Alexandra, it had to be admitted, was exceptionally beautiful that evening. She blossomed under the scrutiny of the room, like one of those plants that flowers when you talk to it.

When she spilled her wine, by flinging an arm out to gesture at the door of the seminar room, not one drop splashed on her shirt, which was silk, and patterned with tiny clocks. It made Dorothy think of Baudelaire and his clock without hands, on which he had written: *It is later than you think.*

"Take *this door*," Alexandra had said, as a master's student hopped up to mop the spill with a napkin. "We use the door every time we come into and leave this room, and we never think about it. But it has a history, and that's what my project is about: rescuing history."

Everything that happened happened in history, so when you rescued history, what did you do with it? Did you put it somewhere else? Where could time be safe from its own ravages? At the end of the meeting Judith held up a plastic cup and offered a toast to Alexandra, who responded with, to Dorothy's consternation, a blush. A blush was the kind of thing you couldn't possibly fake. It was an involuntary rushing of blood to the surface, and yet this blush was so perfectly calibrated to win Judith's affection and to defuse the jealousy of her peers that Dorothy could not help but lean over and whisper to her friend Micah that Alexandra must have taught herself to blush, the way actors can cry, on command. Careful not to look at Dorothy and die laughing, Micah wrote "Work it, girl" across the top of Alexandra's draft; then he took out his pencil and erased it; he did all this without ever taking his eyes off Alexandra or moving his head. Later that year Micah was sexually harassed by the director of graduate studies and left the program. After a brief stint teaching at a private high school, he sold a television pilot about the sex lives of some minor Victorian poets. Last Dorothy had heard, he was living in Silver Lake. The three of them represented the three potential paths of the graduate student: the one who wins, the one who leaves, and the one who does whatever it was Dorothy was doing.

I expect nothing less, I expect nothing less. She read Judith's tweet over and over but never would its expectations extend to her. Dorothy had matured since that colloquium. She no longer wondered if Alexandra had taught herself to blush; rather, she was no longer offended by it. She even found it in herself to admire how Alexandra had found a way to use the system to her advantage, to make a place for herself in the decadent twilight of the profession. Was it Alexandra's fault that she was so finely fitted to the times, so capable of punctually executing the necessary tasks? When Dorothy thought about doors now, she saw that there was plenty to say about their power to include or exclude, their interest as a threshold, the way they could connect insides to outsides and insides to other insides. Without doors there would be no corner offices. There would be nothing special about hopping in through a window, or out of one. But windows were another subject altogether. Windows had to do with transparency, landscape, point of view. Doors had to do with opacity, listening behind, peering through. And of course it mattered how hard they were shut, and on whom.

But Alexandra had never had a door shut in her face, and now she was publishing a book, and would ascend with her iron grasp to the next rung and the next, while Dorothy sat in the waiting room, not working, not writing, bleeding for now the seventh day, wondering if the broker could smell her blood, or only smell her failure.

The door opened and the previous patient, a woman who resembled Dorothy in hair and dress and posture, slunk out, pushing her head forward like a beacon or signal that would arrive in the future half a moment before the rest of her body. Dorothy stood up to take her place, but the therapist, who seemed to materialize from the doorway itself, held up a finger, said, "One minute," and closed the door again. Dorothy sat down. She looked at the ceiling. She looked at the lock screen of her phone. Bonnard's young woman was still hunched over, writing, or maybe she was banging her head against the table.

The door opened again. "Come in," the therapist said, wrapping herself in a huge gray shawl. This therapist always wore this shawl. She was always very cold. It was probably because she was so small—just a wisp of a person, really. She had the full, airbrushed cheeks and the sleepy yet disturbingly penetrating gaze of an eighteenth-century portrait, but if you were to hang her over the mantelpiece in oils, you would want her posed with a hoop in hand or sitting on a pony, like a child. That's how small she was. Her low stature made Dorothy feel affectionate and protective toward her and also like the therapist was another species of female, compact and contained, who in some critical sense could not understand anything about Dorothy's problems, which were ungainly, spilling and shedding everywhere.

Like Dorothy, the second therapist had a PhD. Dorothy appreciated the way the therapist wore her knowledge casually, like one of those loose, shapeless dresses that made some women look elegant and free and others, Dorothy among them, appear vagabond or orphaned. There was even some elegance to how the therapist listened while Dorothy complained about Alexandra—head slightly cocked, legs folded like a crane's. Even more while Dorothy apologized for using their time to talk about Alexandra. The therapist seemed suspended in attention. It was almost as if the therapist were sitting for a portrait, posing for an artist painting the subject of *Listening*, or perhaps *Listening Child*.

"I know I'm supposed to talk about my other therapist with you," Dorothy said. That was the whole point of the second therapist: to talk about why she had sought out a second therapist. "But this just happened."

The second therapist waved a hand—not dismissively or regally, but like she was swatting off whatever guilt was floating around the room before it could become attached to her.

"Since you brought it up," she said. "What did your other therapist say yesterday?"

This was the part that Dorothy had been dreading. "I had to cancel with her," she said. "I had a . . . migraine." A migraine was plausible. People like Dorothy got migraines. The second therapist looked closely at her. "Interesting symptom" was all she said.

Dorothy nodded. It was hot in the room. Too hot for a shawl.

"I know that you know that you can't keep this up forever," the therapist said. Her voice was enticing, like a trap.

Then she leaned forward and adjusted the pillow she sat on, shimmying up and gaining an extra half inch in height. "Two therapists," she said. "Not really recommended. But we'll get to the bottom of what you're doing, and then you won't need to come here anymore."

It was a sad way to look at the world—that as soon as you understood something, you could be rid of it. Maybe that was what Kafka's dog meant by freedom.

"But there is something I need to raise," the therapist said, and catching the startle in Dorothy's eyes, lifted a hand.

"It's about me," she said. "You're not in trouble."

The therapist laughed. Dorothy tried to arrange her face. She tried to make the smile that her therapists did, that little pursed smile that signaled neither approval nor disapproval but simply stated the relationship: *We are in therapy,* was the ultimate meaning of the smile, *and I am a therapist.* The smile seemed gentle and accommodating but it was actually demented. Only someone who had been trained to suppress their humanity, to never reveal their essential self, could do it well. "My podcast," Dorothy heard her second therapist say, and then she heard, "production company," and then, "recording," and then, "premiere."

"I'm sorry," said Dorothy, sludgy in the brain. "Can you say that again?"

For some time, the therapist explained, she had been doing a podcast. On the podcast she talked about the history of psychology and told stories—thoroughly masked and altered, never breaching patient confidentiality—from her years in practice. Dorothy felt like she had just gotten punched in the face. Her therapist had a podcast? How had she not known about this? Did the other patients know? Then more questions: Was she famous? Was she a titan? Did her first therapist listen to the second therapist's podcast? Or was it an amateur podcast, like the kind Rog's friends had? Was the therapist a fundamentally unserious joke of a human being, or was she out of Dorothy's league?

She had come to believe, the therapist was saying, that due to the high cost of individual therapy, she had an ethical duty to serve the public for free.

"Otherwise the profession just becomes helping people who can afford it," she said, wrapping herself snugly—or was it smugly?—in the shawl, which now, Dorothy saw, might actually be a blanket.

Of course in one sense—the literal one, reality, the material world of the possible—Dorothy could afford therapy. She made the payments; they did not bounce. But in another, deeper and more live sense, the sense of should, of what is advisable or correct, the sense that encompassed her lack of savings and safety net and the ongoing drama of her precarious employment, she definitely could not afford it. Did the therapist not get this about her? Wasn't this one of the things they were supposed to be dealing with re: the subject of having two therapists? How was she supposed to be helped if she was so hopelessly misrecognized? She nodded to indicate that the therapist could continue talking and before the nod was even complete she regretted it, fearing that it had somehow committed her to the therapist's false conception of her security, her situation, her life.

Now, the therapist said, the podcast had taken off. The podcast company her agent had paired her with had stipulated that this season consist of recorded sessions with real patients. The market for history, Dorothy thought bitterly, was nothing compared to the market for voyeurism. "Reality" had infiltrated every cultural form.

The word "agent" landed in her ear. Her therapist had an agent.

"You must have questions," the therapist said. "Ask me anything."

Dorothy turned her head to look out the window, but there was no window in this office. Where the window should be was an abstract painting, all white lines and splotches of primary color. Dorothy had never been able to decide if she liked this painting or not. She had no idea if it was real art or if it was hotel art. Probably the therapist could afford real art, but she might have hotel art taste. Dorothy resented that the therapist's painting activated her critical insecurities, not to mention her envy—she had owned many posters but never an actual painting—and she resented that the painting was hung where a window ought to be, so that instead of a hole in the wall granting her the relief/escape of skyline, some sense of life outside the room, she was thrown back in, onto aesthetic questions.

"Do you get paid a lot of money?" Dorothy asked. "For the podcast, I mean."

"Some," said her therapist. A pause. "Shall I tell you how much?"

Dorothy admired the therapist's willingness for candor, but also felt that it was pandering, that the therapist was playing on her financial anxieties in order to distract her from the question they both knew all this was leading to, namely, whether or not the therapist wanted Dorothy to be a guest on the podcast. At the answer—which was, as it could only ever be, "no,"—Dorothy felt a pricking behind the eyeballs. A dopey grin spread helplessly across her face, the clownish tell of embarrassment and rejection. She sat stupidly and silently stumped.

"I've recorded most of the episodes already," said the therapist, proferring what felt like an excuse, and then she pursed her lips in a new way. "Did you want to be on it?" she asked.

"I would have liked to have been asked," Dorothy said to the wall.

At such candor, Dorothy's first therapist would have leaned in excitedly, restraining herself from embracing Dorothy and congratulating her on doing the work. Her second therapist stayed perfectly still. Her pause indicated there was something more she wanted to say but wasn't sure she should, and then she decided to go ahead and say it anyway.

"It's not that you're not sympathetic," she said, "but"—and while she explained something about pathology and privilege and audience and relatability, Dorothy was wondering how many times and with how many other patients the therapist had had this conversation. She was thinking about how much time she, Dorothy, was going to have to waste listening to the podcast, how many hours that she could be reading a book that she would never get back. She felt a burst of anger that they were now going to have to talk about *this* instead of Dorothy's real problems. She knew the therapist was just eating this shit up. This was therapy bread and butter, talking about therapy, wallowing in the transference like two fat pigs on a farm.

Dorothy scratched her nose to hide her mouth and stole a glance at the clock. It was later than she thought. It was almost time to go.

"For the record, Dorothy, *I* find you sympathetic," the therapist said. "But listeners . . ."

Dorothy knew that when she told Rog about this, he would be furious. He would think the therapist was being totally inappropriate. He would say Dorothy should never go back. He would say she shouldn't pay good money to be insulted. But Dorothy wasn't insulted. She was grateful.

"I get it," Dorothy said, aware that the therapist always let her have the last word. "I don't think I'm sympathetic, either."

No matter how hard she tried to arrive just as class was supposed to begin, Dorothy was always early. There was nowhere for her to kill time; she had access to the shared office, a miserable hovel of random paperbacks, abandoned three-ring binders, and someone's framed poster of Van Gogh's sunflowers, a mere two hours a week. Sitting on the bench outside the building made her feel like a loiterer or vagrant. Killing time in the bathroom was an option, but there she risked the forced conviviality of encountering a student at the shared sink, or, god forbid, listening to one of them urinate or worse, or, alternately, knowing that her presence was preventing one of them from urinating or worse. The only thing to do was pass the time in the classroom in such a way that one seemed too loftily engaged in preparation to be interrupted, or to hold oneself so still that one disappeared into the scene, like a hunter in a blind, or a piece of furniture.

The classroom was a modern, largish square that had been furnished by someone who hated wood. The plasticky conjoined desk chairs were organized around the focal point of a whiteboard and eraser (there were never any markers). Dorothy shuffled papers and stared at the highlighted passages without absorbing their meaning while the students rolled in, talking loudly or frantically enjoying a few last minutes with their phones before class began. Today a student named Danielle, a redhead with a greyhound tattooed on the inside of her wrist and a crisp, dismissive style, was presenting on Silvan Tomkins's concepts of shame-humiliation and contempt-disgust. Dorothy disliked Danielle and was also a little afraid of her. Danielle was always eager to participate, often had her hand in the air before Dorothy had finished speaking, but her contribution to discussion was inevitably deflating. She found most of the readings Dorothy assigned "ridiculous," a word she said in a tone not of scorn but of exasperated disbelief and pity. Dorothy had met many students who dismissed the assigned work out of insecurity or confusion or insecurity over their own confusion, who hated what they did not understand, but Danielle was different. She was sharp and hostile. She understood the authors' arguments perfectly well, only she felt sorry for them, to have misspent so much life making them. Danielle was unsparing in her separation of things into categories of useful or useless, and while Dorothy's whole useless existence, which failed to rise to the glorious level of the uselessness of art, and instead languished in abject futility, was dismissed by Danielle, Dorothy grudgingly admired the surety with which Danielle pursued her passion for utility. Swaggering, superior, confident youth—Dorothy marveled at it. It gave her the feeling she had when she looked at pictures of icebergs. They would melt—they were melting—but oh! They had been glorious in their prime.

The words "shame-humiliation" and "contempt-disgust" sounded foreign, like poetry, in Danielle's mouth. Danielle was a human being, and so of course must have experienced shame, humiliation, contempt, disgust, and all their combinations, but she seemed to have no personal relationship to what she was talking about. She recited Tomkins's words in the informative tone one uses for driving directions or a recipe: "Though terror speaks to life and death, and distress makes of the world a vale of tears, yet shame strikes deepest into the heart of man."

From the back of the room came a cough. Dorothy, assuming someone was about to present an objection to "man" as the universal subject, started preparing a speech on how we had to cut the past a little bit of slack—not to excuse it, but we couldn't spend the whole class period adjudicating what we already knew was wrong when there were concepts to learn, and she was aware that her belief that concepts could be separated or at least salvaged from their context put her out of step with the next generation, but—"Sorry," said Ryder, looking mortified. "It went down the wrong pipe."

There was no bottle of water or coffee or other beverage on the desk in front of Ryder, so Dorothy was not sure what had gone down the pipe, but she didn't think it was her business to interrogate. It was impossible to bring a moment like this with any student to a satisfactory conclusion, but with Ryder, Dorothy was always aware of an extra layer of bad feeling, a skein of accusation and judgment. Ryder had face-blindness, a fact that Dorothy had learned after the first class of the semester, when he had approached her desk while she was pretending to be organizing her papers to accuse her of failing to remember him. "I was in your Introduction to the Major last fall," Ryder had said that day. "You probably don't remember me, because I have face-blindness."

In fact Dorothy had not remembered Ryder, though she didn't see what his having face-blindness had to do with it, unless it was that being face-blind caused Ryder to recede in social situations and avoid drawing attention to himself, and so the face-blindness, which caused him to forget others, made him himself forgettable. She should have admitted it right away, but instead she had pretended to know him, and the conversation had continued until Ryder dropped enough information for Dorothy to realize that he was confusing her with another Dorothy who taught in the department—it was *her* Introduction to the Major course Ryder had taken. Now Dorothy trod lightly around Ryder, anxious that her lie, which she justified as tact, might be discovered. It wouldn't be so terrible if he confronted her privately, but she dreaded being made an example of online or in front of the class, a spectacle that she feared precisely because she knew she deserved it.

"Sorry," Ryder said again.

"Can I go on?" Danielle asked, glaring around the room.

"Let's keep going," said Dorothy.

Danielle explained, glancing up now and again from her paper to receive nods of confirmation from Dorothy, that, according to Tomkins, shame occurred when some positive or interesting experience had been interrupted. Suddenly there was a dinging noise, the noise of a phone receiving a text message, and Ryder fumbled to silence the device.

"Sorry again," he said, and some people laughed.

Danielle repeated her last sentence: Shame is provoked by a positive experience, she said. It involves some pleasure or joy that turns into its opposite, becomes unacceptable, or is not shared. Now Danielle was no longer giving directions. Now she sounded like a television anchor delivering news of a heat wave in a foreign country in which some old people had died—sympathetic, but abstract. She was an observer, fundamentally unaffected by the tragedy, which was local in nature. Around the circle of desks Dorothy noted expressions of boredom, confusion, and the kind of rapid stuttery nodding that indicated artificial stimulation. She began to doubt that it had been a good idea, asking these undergraduates to read Silvan Tomkins. You could do so much damage, giving someone a book at the wrong time. You could prevent them from loving it, or—and this could be worse—make them love it too much, or too stupidly. They might waste years of their lives because they read the wrong book at the right time, or the right book at the wrong time, or the wrong book at the wrong time. Teaching was an enormous responsibility. Dorothy hated it.

Danielle sat down.

"Great job!" Dorothy said.

The discussion that followed was better than Dorothy had imagined it would be. Ryder didn't cough again and Dorothy almost allowed herself to believe that no one was checking their email while she talked. Toward the end, someone raised the meaning of "shameless," and whether certain "shameless" behaviors or disclosures indicated that a person took pleasure in their actions/approved of themselves or were merely compulsive. To what extent was shame a social good, etc. "Why do people reveal their worst selves?" Dorothy asked the class. "Do they want to die, or to survive death?"

They looked blankly at her. The clock dismissed them.

"I mean, is 'shameless' the opposite of 'shameful'?" Dorothy shouted to their retreating heads.

In the bathroom after class, she reviewed the points she had failed to make, the things she should have said, if only she had thought them in time. Her panty liner was smudged with what looked like a brownish fingerprint. She unstuck the liner and smelled its iron smell. Then she rolled up the liner, threw it away in the empty silver canister, peeled the backing off a new one, and smoothed it down so it adhered to her cotton underwear. She peeked in the silver canister and saw that the used panty liner had unfurled a little. She felt a pang of regret for the next user of the canister. She opened the camera on her phone to look at her hair and waited for the bathroom to empty before she unlocked the door and arrived five minutes late to the Apocalypse. No one seemed to mind. The students were thrilled by Edwards's meteorological descriptions of the rising waters of wrath, and the hotness of the flames. Jessie— she was there, oddly; the action must have been canceled or postponed—called it "surprisingly relevant." Dorothy tried to tell them that hell had always been hot, but they weren't listening, and then teaching was over for another day.

On the train home, a man dressed in rags entered the subway car to scream the sad story of his life. His neck was mole covered and splotchy. His tatters had once been a navy-colored suit—long rents in the pants exposed hairy, frail legs—and his scraggle of beard was discolored as city snow. He clutched his fate around himself like a stole.

Dorothy was reading "The Rime of the Ancient Mariner" to prepare for tomorrow's Intro course, but even had she not been reading a poem about the sea, she would still have seen the ragman as a tragic shipwreck, a dehydrated, sunburnt, three-quarters-starved captain clinging to the last splintering boards of his lifeboat. He rocked around the subway car, pointing to each passenger and enumerating his debts. To the man in the backward cap, he said: "Divorce court." To the woman wearing an infant, he said: "Child support." To an elderly couple examining their printed map, he said:

"The staph infection I got on March 15, 2015, at Methodist hospital." This last item Dorothy thought suspiciously specific, but even if the date was the mariner's attempt at a reality effect, it didn't mean he had never gotten a staph infection. And maybe it was true. Dates had an odd and uneven quality. You never could tell ahead of time what times you would remember but you were likely to remember some of them.

The woman wearing the infant nudged her husband, a handsome man who had overexercised his upper body. In village life he would have been a butcher. He peeked into his wallet and put it away. *All twenties,* he mouthed to his wife. She shrugged as if to say, *We tried*.

The mariner was already surviving his worst-case scenario. His life of extreme deprivation was a rebuke to Dorothy's comfortable precarity, her pathology and privilege. All through the car people turned from him, because he exposed the indefensible arbitrariness of fate, and because on some level they knew that only a few horrible turns of events separated them from him, and either they could not bear to see what they might have been, or they could not bear to face their own lack of compassion. They could not look at him but he would be looked at. They would not speak to him but he would speak.

The mariner wore appalling shoes. They had split into flaps that opened and shut like the mouths of crocodiles, or sock puppets. He shuffled to the end of the car and turned back, as if he had arrived on a podium, to address them as a group. (They had not been a group, but addressed as such became one; such, Dorothy reflected, is the power of a speaker.) He had written a movie, he announced, but his friend stole the idea and made a million dollars. He had written a novel. He had talked to some Israelis the day before 9/11 and that's how he knew to stay uptown that day. Before his entrance, Coleridge's words had seemed singsongy and faraway, like a hymn whose lines you repeat unthinkingly. Now Dorothy felt its horror, its abjection. She saw the true meaning of the wedding guest's situation: what the poet means by *he cannot choose but hear*. It was not just her ordinary obtuseness, and her distance from the quotidian concerns of the nineteenth century, that had alienated her through so many readings from the poem. It was not just the limitations of mind and history that had prevented her from truly loving the poem. It wasn't because she wasn't a sailor. It was because *no one* wants to listen to the Ancient Mariner. Resistance, she saw with growing excitement, had not prevented her from some authentic aesthetic experience; resistance *was* the aesthetic experience. Dorothy was not a failed reader of this poem, she was a member of the poem's community; she was the ideal reader! She watched as the woman with the baby followed her frugal mate to the other end of the car, alternating hands on the poles over-head like she was swinging herself along a monkey bar. Up and down the aisle headphones materialized out of pockets and bags, plugging up ears that had previously been exposed. The fear of Coleridge's guest, the longing to get away, passed down like the squeeze of a hand.

She forced herself to look into his wild milky eyes as she handed the mariner a dollar. Then, at the next stop, she stuck her thumb in the book, stepped off the train, and darted into the next car. She turned around and the mariner was before her. He had gone through the connecting doors inside the train, which Dorothy never did, because she was afraid to die.

She pressed against the closed doors, trying to be smaller than she was. The mariner leaned close to her and asked her shoulder for a dollar. He waited calmly while she fished one out of her wallet. A thought ribboned its way through her busy mind—*This man is an albatross around my neck*—but, she knew, the words didn't mean anything, they had merely become unloosed from the poem. The bellowing capitals stretched out from beneath her fingers: *I shot the ALBA-TROSS.* And then, without any warning, Dorothy thought of Richard, who she had not thought of for many years, because Richard had always reminded her of an albatross: wounded, waddling, determined, and white, with yellow hair, like an albatross's hard, curved beak.

Richard was a student in Dorothy's sixth grade class. In addition to being albino he was legally blind and obese. Dorothy, who in those days wore a cross around her neck, had tried to be kind to Richard in small ways. For example, she never held her nose when he brushed past on his way to the pencil sharpener. But he was viciously teased by the others. One day when Richard was absent the teachers herded all the students into the gym, handed out cardboard glasses that simulated Richard's poor vision, pointed to an obstacle course, and said, "Now run that." There were foam stairs, a mat maze, and a rope to swing from. The last challenge involved the gym teacher throwing soft balls and demanding the students catch. By the end of the period a few girls were crying and someone had a bloodied nose. Dorothy did pretty well, injury-wise, but that was because she took it slow and visualized Richard the whole time. She tried to move like he did, with a heaving, heavy grace.

The teasing got worse after that. Dorothy was a bird kid, and a few times she stuffed anonymous notes of encouragement decorated with drawings of seabirds into Richard's locker, but one of the teachers caught her, and told her to stop. Eventually Richard stopped attending her school. Dorothy wasn't sure if he transferred to a specialized school or if his family moved away, perhaps for unrelated reasons—a job transfer, or a grandparent died and they inherited a bigger house. She hoped it was an inheritance.

For a long time she worried about Richard's future. What sort of career was he suited for? He looked uncomfortable behind a desk, but he probably wasn't allowed to operate heavy machinery. Would he be able to live independently as an adult, or would his mother have to take care of him? Dorothy pictured Richard at retirement age, living in his childhood bedroom, eating his mother's food. Were the walls painted with footballs or trains? Would he never fly away? She was twelve, but a mature twelve. She wondered about Richard's mother. In Dorothy's mind Richard's mother was unhappy but kept her unhappiness a secret to protect Richard, who she loved more than life itself. Dorothy had always been frightened by the maternal capacity to love fiercely, to be caught in the grip of love. She became obsessed with the image of Richard as her son, and it frightened her. She spoke to no one about these things but God knew. God knew that she did not want to have a child like Richard. God knew she did not want a Richard, and because He knew this, He was sure to give her one, to teach her a lesson about love. Her soul, she miserably acknowledged, as she lay in the dark of her adolescent room, staring up at a ceiling beplasticked with sickly green stars, would be enriched, and she would have the blessing of a compassionate life. The love would come to her. But she did not want it. She did not want to learn a lesson, even if it meant having a blessed, enriched soul.

Dorothy did not *believe,* in an active way, that God *intended* to intervene in the genetic makeup of her offspring.

Only people with no religious feeling used words like "believe."

Dorothy didn't have to "believe" that God was going to do this, any more than she "believed" that the earth was round or that water was wet. The facts of her life, as all life, were subject to rules. She didn't make the rules.

People who grew up secular liked to say that they couldn't believe in an unjust God. But Dorothy saw evidence of injustice all around.

Dorothy was aware, reflecting on the situation, that she had not been truly empathetic toward Richard, that she had not been a friend. She was aware that she had been obsessed with Richard's difference. She had not considered him in his full personhood. She had not actually spoken to him. She had not signed her letters. She had pitied Richard, and been afraid of him. He, who was not even monstrous, who was just a large, friendless kid with some learning and hygiene issues, had stood in her immature mind for all the monstrosity that a body could produce, for all the aberrations from the norm, for how children are so totally out of their mothers' control, for how the future cannot be contained by the past. She wondered what dreams her own mother had for her that had gone unfulfilled. Who her mother would have chosen her to be, had she been given the choice.

The mariner toddled to the middle of the car on his appalling, open-jawed shoes and started his tale of woe from the top. He had written a movie. He had written a novel. Jesus, even this insane panhandler had finished his book! Dorothy looked down at the poem. She didn't like Coleridge. He was supernatural, pompous. *God save thee, ancient Mariner!* she read, *From the fiends, that plague thee thus!—*

Why look'st thou so?—With my cross-bow
I shot the ALBATROSS.

She did not want to be the mariner, forcing the story of her shame on unwilling ears, yet she could not deny that only by telling his tale was the mariner released from his shame. But to be the mariner—to hold the attention of others—involved some combination of tragedy and gruesome charisma, some sheer skill, that she lacked. She had a terrible vision of the mariner's lofted crossbow and Richard's large, soft body, cocooned in the leather jacket he always wore in a doomed attempt to appear tough, tumbling to the ground and bouncing gently on impact. She got off the train at the next stop and waited on the platform, trying, and failing, to shake this disturbing image from her mind.

On the twelfth day of bleeding she went back to the ob-gyn. The receptionist greeted her with the same bland disinterest she had exhibited when Dorothy was carrying the blight. But what had seemed on earlier appointments like unwelcoming sternness Dorothy saw now as studied neutrality. The receptionist did not register any knowledge of her situation. This was not ignorance, but tact, and something more—a survival skill. To take interest in one patient's blight would be to take interest in the plight of all. There would be no end of it.

Rog was at work. Dorothy took a seat by the watercooler and put her bag on the chair next to her and opened her copy of *Rebecca.* It was comfort rereading, but as Dorothy had no memory for events, it offered also the additional pleasure of suspense. Her problems with recall were a liability in the classroom, insofar as it took valuable time to be always rereading the books she assigned, but on the plus side, it made it easier to relate to the fresh excitement of her students. It was the closest she got to *living in the moment*—reliving moments she had lived before.

The office was split into two levels, and as Dorothy was finding her place on the page a skinny woman came up from below and fumbled to open the gate at the top of the stairs. A heavily pregnant woman admonished her toddler to stay in place and went over to help the girl. The skinny woman intrigued Dorothy. She was draped in white, like a beachcomber or cult member, and her hair was shorn like a spring sheep. She might have been in the early weeks of pregnancy, or due for an annual pap, or the victim of a nasty UTI, or suffering from stage I or II cervical cancer. There was no way to tell from the outside what was happening inside. Illness could be asymptomatic. The sickest people could glow with false health—red lips, dewy cheeks. This was the whole thing about "showing." Life and death, viability and unviability, persisted under cover of darkness. It took time to thicken in the middle. When you most needed a seat, you could not ask for one. And then once you were showing, you were the show.

The woman in white took a seat opposite Dorothy and busied herself with the forms on the blue clipboard. Anything could be going on with her but someone wearing that much white was probably not continuously bleeding, or else she was exceedingly confident in the quality of her feminine-hygiene products. The doctor was running late, as usual. Dorothy read half a page of *Rebecca*. It was odd that no one in this book had children. Perhaps that was the meaning of the double. By reproducing an individual, the double interfered with the reproduction of a generation.

A Pretenders song ended and the energetic opening chords of "Second Hand News" picked up speed, like sonic horses leaning into a bend in the track. From a list of all music in the world that had ever been recorded, someone had chosen this music to play here, in this environment. Or rather, someone had chosen music like this music; they had selected a genre, and the computer had done the rest. This experience, like so many in the modern world, had been curated with the minimum of human intention/agency. The feelings she was feeling—an uptick in happiness and energy, a humming mood at once new and familiar—had been factored into the choice and yet were also a happenstance of the shuffle. What was worse—the institutionality of silence or the institutionality of noise?

Was being left to one's own devices better or worse than being coerced into pleasure?

The light was gentle and emanating. If there were bulbs in the fixtures they were invisible within the frosted glass. A nurse with a high forehead and bleached streak came through the reception area dancing. She opened a drawer, took something out, and danced away. Perhaps she had chosen the station, or perhaps she was lucky in a different way—to be so entirely suited to her surroundings. She had found her place! Dorothy hoped she would never lose it. Neon pink cows with big moony eyes silently lowed from the wallpaper like rejects from Warhol's studio. Or maybe it was an actual Warhol pattern? Dorothy didn't know if the cow motif was supposed to be funny but it felt inappropriate just the same. Pregnant people already felt like cows, didn't they? Or maybe when you saw the cows you were supposed to think of milk. Wasn't that offensive to people who used formula, or who weren't pregnant at all?

Mother whales make two hundred liters of milk a day. Gaby had texted her that piece of trivia when she was first breastfeeding. Oddly, that wasn't the only animal mammary knowledge that Dorothy had at her fingertips. She also knew that elephant seals nurse for one month, after which they leave the pups to fend for themselves. Some of the pups don't fend. They hang around the beach and find other mothers to nurse them and when those mothers leave find other mothers and repeat as long as they can until no one nurses them and they die of starvation. She had learned that on a trip to a marine hospital that Rog had insisted on visiting last year while they were driving up the Northern California coastline.

The marine hospital was awful. It was like a jail for seals. Dorothy didn't understand why it had to exist, or why Rog wanted to go there. And why didn't the authorities let the seals die on the beaches? she said while they stood on the cement overlook peering down into the metal cages. It wasn't like they were endangered.

"You're heartless" is how Rog responded. Later, over beers on the cold gray Sausalito sand he had added, "And you have no grasp of optics. People don't want to see a pile of dead baby seals when they're out for a walk."

Rog had misunderstood. It wasn't that Dorothy was heartless or unsavvy about the media or unable to imagine the pressures of running a nonprofit. It was that she didn't believe that everyone or everything could be rescued. There was something neurotic, she said, in the avoidance of death. Rog countered that there was a difference between avoiding death and ameliorating needless suffering.

"But why would we overrule their mothers?" asked Dorothy. "Don't mothers know best?"

Dorothy shifted in the plastic seat. She rubbed her shoulder, her neck. She had to stop hunching. If she wasn't careful she would become one of those ancient horizontal city-dwellers who walk bent in half, twisting their decrepit necks to the side to avoid the cracks in the sidewalk. She would have said she was exhausted, but she had to admit, as she pressed her fingers into the hard knot of compacted, agonized muscle, admiring and fearing the resistance she encountered, that she had lost a sense of what it felt like to be normally energetic. *Was* she tired? How *should* a person feel? Maybe everyone felt like this—twisted and sore, blunted. Maybe this was the standard. She had no sense of what was reasonable, of what she could reasonably expect, of what, therefore, could fail to measure up. The last time she had felt truly awake was the morning after the miscarriage. After the sanguinary deluge and the dark deep oxy sleep came a fabulous dawn rush—an explosion of physical and mental energy. She sprang out of bed! She could not remember ever in her life having felt so good! The rot had been flushed away and with it the dread; she was risen.

That morning, when she was still heavily bleeding and wearing maximum absorbency sanitary napkins, Rog took the day off and they went to the Guggenheim to see the Hilma af Klint retrospective that everyone was talking about. Rog had wanted her to stay in bed to rest, but she insisted. The top of her head had been taken off. She had to get out. At the museum she had so much to say; she could not control the tempo of her speech. She scanned the paintings as one takes stock of a crowd but mostly she wanted to *talk about how good she felt*. How she was living, once again, in open time. Open time that was not for anything. People lived in this time without knowing what it was, without knowing it had a name. She had journeyed to other times and was back to tell the tale.

"I guess we dodged a bullet," said Rog, eyes fixed on the wall text. "It sounds like you really didn't want to have a baby."

"That's not fair," said Dorothy. "That's not what I said."

Rog read out loud. Af Klint, a Swedish mystic, had been a gifted draughtswoman who made money with scientific drawings. She co-illustrated a book about horse surgery. He gestured to a realistic drawing of a dog. Dorothy found the neediness of the dog inexpressibly moving. That the woman who drew that dog had also invented her own abstract symbolic language was impressive. They paused in front of a series of huge canvases that af Klint had painted for a temple that had never been built. Everything was round, squiggle, flower. An orange and a blue circle overlapped just slightly, the yellow meeting point suggesting only the narrowest ledge of mutual comprehension.

"Do you think," Dorothy said, "that she felt her life was unfinished? Because her work couldn't be seen the way she had intended for it to be seen?"

By open time, she added, she meant time in contrast to reproductive time. Reproductive time, she said, following Rog across the proscenium, had been waiting time: waiting for the second line to appear, and then waiting for the OB appointment, and then waiting for the follow-up appointment, and then waiting for the Cytotec to kick in, and then waiting for the second Cytotec to kick in. It hadn't worked the first time. She'd had to do it twice. You had to push the tablet all the way up to the second knuckle, way into the vaginal canal so it could be absorbed into the walls there. Waiting time was sitting time, lying down time, sitting up again time, for hours, it was watching television while checking your phone time, it was alone time, texting with Rog, Rog was at work—

"I got home as soon as I could," said Rog. "You know I didn't mean to be late."

In fairness, he had arrived before the onset of the terrible abdominal convulsions, which felt like something tight and compacted inside splitting a little bit, and then a lot, like Dorothy was a seismic zone and there was a tectonic plate inside her mantle grinding against itself. She managed with a heating pad and the painkiller, and by lying on her side, and moaning, out loud, like an injured animal, an abandoned seal. Pain effectively removed the need to think about anything else, it removed inhibitions around itself, it made itself the priority. In that sense it was relaxing; there were no decisions to be made. You knew where you stood with pain. She wasn't sure how long the pain went on but it was a relief when it started, it represented the start that would also be the end. She would never have called them labor pains—how embarrassing, to claim them as such, how disrespectful—but she knew, technically, that they were. What to call them, though? In what category of pain did they belong, and if they didn't have a category, did they even exist? Rank this pain on a scale of one to ten, Rog had said, concerned. Dorothy had just looked at him, like, *Why?*

There was blood. The doctor had told her it would be "heavy," that she would "soak" through sanitary napkins, but those were just words, letter and phoneme combinations, liability coverage. There was too much blood, it must have been coming from somewhere other than inside her own body, and yet where else could it have originated? Then there was more. It seeped through the plastic coating on the underside of the pad, sagging in huge red maps. It had a dull metallic smell. The smell was big, like a cave; you could live inside the smell. Rog repeated how unfair it was that Dorothy had to suffer this way because she was a woman but Dorothy did not understand why you would want not to suffer this way. This way was all-encompassing. Was there another way? Again and again Dorothy changed the sanitary napkins, rolling them up into huge scrolls and stacking them in the trash can, and fell asleep, exhausted, dreamless, undefended. Where had Rog slept? In the bed?

"Yes," he said, breaking eye contact with a black swan to look at her. "Right next to you."

Once or twice Rog tried to turn the conversation from Dorothy's sheer insane joy to be alive back to the paintings, geometric abstractions in pink and orange and other colors that Dorothy had seen in museums, but spread out as accents, never in this volume and density—never this much pink, this close together—but Dorothy did not especially want to talk about the paintings, and wished she had gone to see them some other day, by herself.

Of one, he said, "How feminist," an anachronism that made Dorothy extremely angry.

"We need to live *in our own time*" was all she could get out.

Usually Dorothy didn't bother to linger over art. If she was going to see something, she saw it right away, especially if a face was concerned, or if the canvas was busy or freighted with objects. These paintings were different. They were empty for the most part, but it seemed like the more she looked the more she could see of them, or maybe she meant she could go deeper into them, like a portal, or perhaps like the feeling of DMT, which she had read was like rushing toward a door in your mind. It was like the time that Dorothy and Rog had taken ayahuasca, in a salsa-dancing studio that overlooked a gas station, but the shaman, made nervous by the size of the group, had intentionally watered down the dose, and although Dorothy had dutifully puked up her dinner into a pink plastic bucket and felt a rapid mental rushing through space like what she had read was associated with DMT, when she got to the door it was locked, and wouldn't open. The paintings of Hilma af Klint were exciting and frustrating like weak ayahuasca. Dorothy rushed toward them expectantly and though they didn't repel her they also didn't transport her and they themselves did not change or go anywhere else. They were more of what they had been. She could never have written a paper about them. She could not think about them; she could only think near them.

Dorothy didn't bring up the ayahuasca with Rog. It still made him angry to think about. He still wanted his money back. "If there were a better business bureau for drugs to complain to, I would" had been his first and last take on the experience.

At the museum, Rog said again how feminine the paintings were, how "female." Dorothy nodded but knew he was wrong. They were cold, precise, genderless messages from the far reaches of outer space, from a place where there were lines and pyramids and crystals but no bodies and no blood. As they ascended the spiral ramp Dorothy felt herself attaining the higher ground after all, not in one painting but in the aggregate of all the paintings. She was leaving her body behind, reaching closer to heaven or the transcendent heavenly sphere. The air was thinner up here. She felt a joy to be leaving her body but also expected, from the highest point in the museum, to feel a joy when she reunited with her body at the bottom level. By the time they had descended and exited the building, however, she had slipped back into her body without being aware of it, and when they stopped for lunch Dorothy ate all the bread on the table, and all the food on her plate, and when she was uncomfortably full, she was sad there wasn't any more to eat.

Dorothy's pocket dinged. She let her book close and fished the phone out of her jacket. Gaby was having a panic attack, or thought she might be. Without activating any process in her cerebral cortex—without choosing, deliberating, or think-ing—Dorothy's thumbs ricocheted over the screen.

> Dorothy: What are your symptoms?
> Gaby: . . .
> Dorothy: Are you OK?
> Gaby: I'm freaking out.

Dorothy didn't understand why Gaby texted these things instead of calling. Was Dorothy supposed to call back? Or would calling be aggressive, a way of raising the stakes, and ought she respect the medium in which Gaby had initiated the conversation? Then again, maybe Gaby hadn't chosen to text at all—her fingers, presumably, were as automated as Dorothy's.

> Gaby: I think my marriage is ending.
> Gaby: He holds Sherman wrong.
> Dorothy: What do you mean wrong
> Gaby: I can just tell he doesn't like it! I'm his mother so
> Gaby: I know!
> Gaby: I'm crying sooooo hard
> Dorothy: It's ok you'll be ok

Gaby: I think I'm hyperventilating.
Gaby: What is hyperventilating like?
Dorothy: I think it's breathing really fast?

Gaby's words intruded or heedlessly barged their way into the calm bovine space of the waiting room like someone who did not respect the need to schedule an appointment. Dorothy had the unpleasant sensation of falling between worlds, or more precisely, of being divided and conquered across multiple planes. Gaby was somewhere else, not so far by miles but it would have taken forty minutes at least to travel to her. But space, which had begun to constrict two centuries ago with the invention of the bicycle and the railroad, had been in the last decade entirely obliterated; it was less than an afterthought, it was a dim cultural memory, it was telling stories around the campfire. The psychic effect of texting was to introduce a foreign and yet highly localized weather pattern, as if it had suddenly begun hailing on Dorothy's head, and the other patients were blinking in sunshine. And yet since the words came from Dorothy's own phone, lit up on the book on her lap, it was perhaps more like the words were coming from Dorothy herself—like the weather was coming from Dorothy herself—like *she* was the intrusion. But that only made it harder to understand how to prevent it from happening.

Dorothy: Calm down!!!
Dorothy: Sorry, I know that isn't helpful.
Dorothy: What do you do when you need to feel calm? Can you meditate? Count down? My therapists tell me to count down.
Gaby: Snuggle the baby but
Dorothy: Well one of them tells me to count down. The other one says just to do it if it works for you. Does it work for you
Gaby: . . .
Dorothy: I read an article about meditating. Should I send it Y/ N?

Gaby: . . .

Gaby: . . .

Gaby: The baby is with the babysitter

Dorothy: Can you look at a picture of the baby? Send me a picture and we can look at it together!

Gaby: . . .

Gaby: . . .

Gaby: I can't decide, I'm freaking out which one is the Best oen to send???

Dorothy: It doesn't matter, never mind, just look at all of them.

Dorothy: Don't send me any.

Gaby: Don't you want to see??

Dorothy: Yes OF COURSE, I am just trying to help remove some of the indecision here.

Dorothy: Hello? Are you OK? Do you have a Xanax or something?

Gaby: I DO NOT NEED TO GO ON ANTIDEPRESSANTS

Dorothy: That's not what I mean.

Dorothy: Do you KNOW anyone who has a Xanax?

Dorothy: It's insane, how can you not know someone who has a Xanax?

Dorothy: I took a Xanax once, it really helped.??????

Gaby: I'm okay now

Dorothy: Are you sure?

Gaby: Stalin

Gaby: . . .

Gaby: ducking autocorrect.

Gaby: DUCKING autocorrect.

Gaby: [Munch *Scream* emoji] It autocorrected "Stalin" to "Stalin"

Gaby: OMFG

Gaby: "srsly"

The nurse called Dorothy's first and last name, which felt

excessive and possibly illegal, perhaps even a HIPAA violation, and Dorothy dropped her phone into her bag without saying goodbye. The nurse ushered her to the scale in the hallway, where Dorothy quickly removed her shoes before she could get tricked into being heavier than she was. In the cold, small exam room she was bound with the pressurized cuff, which squeezed and sighed wearily. The nurse—not the one with the streak who had danced into the reception area, but her stocky, brusque colleague, with a face hard as granite—roughly returned the cuff to its handle on the wall, where it again resumed the odd, artificial appearance of a gallery display, and told Dorothy to undress and wait.

The purple robe grazed the tops of her thighs. The short hairs on her legs rose and bristled like a creature readying itself to fight. At the first appointment there had been a circle on the screen, pulsing, like an amoeba. Rog had been there. He had been standing somewhere in the background to her side while the doctor pushed the jellied wand inside. They had silently watched the quivering circle blob around in the moonless dark. It felt eerie and sacred. They were bearing witness to primeval genesis, reactions in the hot swamp, the dark art of cellular division. Dorothy hadn't known what it was supposed to look like so she didn't think that anything was wrong. She didn't necessarily think anything was right, either. She wasn't thinking about things being right or wrong. It was like looking at a math equation. It signified truth but you didn't catch the details. It seemed plausible that life would begin this way, as a circle palpitating in the shadows.

Then the doctor pulled the wand out and handed Dorothy a napkin to clean herself with. It wasn't like she had been fucking a phallus-shaped camera that inconsiderately came inside her, but it wasn't *not* like that. The screen went black. We have to wait and see, the doctor said. They should come back in a week.

"Was that not what we were supposed to see?" asked Rog.

The doctor shook her head. She wasn't sure. It might be that the ovum was blighted or it might be that their timing was off. If the timing was off then everything was fine but they were one week earlier, development-wise, than they had believed. That would explain the shape, or lack thereof. For weeks Dorothy had been anticipating tests, genetics, sequencing, the whole ethical quagmire of defects and norms. But there might not be anything to test.

Her urine had registered pregnancy. The blood draw concurred. The right chemicals were surging. Dorothy did not know whether to respect this chemical optimism or to condemn its stupidity. One had to be pregnant in several ways, it appeared, to be pregnant at all: Pregnancy proper involved the manufacture of hormones and the development of a biosphere as well as the ontogenesis of a life-form acquiring mass, gills, limbs, a frontal cortex, ears, and genitals. A baby grew a distinctively enlarged forehead, tiny hands. But it was possible for a body to thicken and prepare an environment for an organism that chose not to develop. It was possible for a body to be pregnant without a pregnancy developing.

She passed another nauseated week ordering tonic water and lime in a whisper. At the next week's ultrasound, the embryo had made no progress. There was no head, no fetal cranium, only the same amoeba-like circle. It squiggled with false breath. Dorothy was a week older but the ovum was the same age. *Circle of life,* Dorothy thought, and then that song was stuck in her head for the rest of the day.

"We need to get it out," the doctor had said. *It.*

"What would have happened to me in the time before sonograms?" Dorothy had asked. She always wanted to know how she would have fared in a pre-technological moment. She imagined being poisoned by an embryo rotting inside her while she baked bread, martyrishly, to nourish the five other children who would survive in penury after her death. The doctor said she would probably have hemorrhaged at some point, which might have been dangerous but not necessarily fatal. She said not to wait too long, because she still might hemorrhage.

"Some women prefer to do the procedure here," the doctor said.

"If I do it at home, will I see a tiny hand or foot come out?" Dorothy asked.

The doctor said no. "Remember?" she added gently. "It's just tissue."

So that, in a sense, was the whole problem. The lack of hands and feet.

Now she was back for the follow-up. As promised, no extremities, no "parts" of any kind, had been expelled. Dorothy pushed in and out against the maroon socks that covered the metal footrests. Were they fleece, future ocean waste, and did it matter, and to whom? She lifted a leg to cross over her other leg and some of the paper on the chair came up with her leg and ripped. Was she too damp or did paper always stick to skin? The longer she sat there, the more she felt like an unwitting participant in a sociological study. She had not read the release forms carefully enough. What did they say?

Was she supposed to get dressed and leave? There was no clock in the room. It was later than she thought. What did all this waiting prove—was it a test of patience, or was there a moment when a person had to cut her losses and accept that she had been abandoned, God was dead, etc.? She hopped off the table, and while she was crouched down, holding the useless cotton robe against her breasts, aware even in her solitude that the robe would not cover her if she bent too far over, the door opened. Dorothy hadn't located her phone so she didn't have to drop it.

"Hi," she said.

"Hi," said the doctor.

Dorothy's doctor had a face like a sunflower, round and bursting open, and a musical voice. Dorothy trusted her more than she had ever trusted a doctor. She was Gaby's doctor, too. Gaby had been horrified by the doctors Dorothy had seen when she was on her grad student insurance—the student dentists, even the specialists. Once, in the throes of a six-week-long urinary tract infection contracted in a rare period of promiscuity, an off-campus urologist had commanded Dorothy to open her legs, asked her what she did for a living, and then, without waiting for a reply, inserted a catheter. "It's quicker than having you pee in a cup," he said by way of explanation, "and less messy." One leak made it harder to control any others and the tears had rolled down Dorothy's face, lukewarm and sloppy, and her nose ran, too, as her own urine, no longer under her volition, flowed into a bag, while the doctor scolded her. "Don't you urinate after intercourse?" he had asked, and Dorothy would never forget the way he said "intercourse," it was so foul and bleak. The truth was no, she had not leapt out of bed to urinate after intercourse, she had instead enjoyed the feeling of being held by another human being, and this was what she got for it: burning pain and humiliation. She had searched the nurse's eyes for sympathy, assuming a woman would come to her aid, but the nurse had only frowned and, when the bag was filled with its incriminatingly yellow liquid, sealed it with a loud and authoritative zip. In that waiting room they had not played any music at all.

The ultrasound machine hummed and whined to life. The ob-gyn reached for the lights without standing up. Once she sat down she never stood up. She did everything while stationed on the wheeled backless stool that kept her at, roughly, baby-catching height. It seemed like it would be awkward to be rolling around down there but there was something dignified and smooth in all of her movements.

Again, as she had done on each of the previous visits, she slowly and firmly pushed the jellied wand up into the cavity of Dorothy's body. Dorothy tried not to clench her jaw but did anyway; she exhaled a little, trying to make more room. On the monitor rustled shadows resembling tangled sheaves of seagrass. These were not clots but they were thicknesses, tissue strands, and they still needed to be coaxed out. They were lingering—malingering, even.

"It will be fine," the doctor said in her high, musical voice. "If you're worried, you can come back in for another scan, but it should be fine."

"You said the bleeding would only last ten days," Dorothy said. She was trying to be funny but it came out petulant, more accusing than wry, and worried.

"Those are averages," the doctor said, in a tone that was not condescending but matter-of-fact, free of condemnation, totally forgiving, absolutely accepting. It was the voice of a mother—not Dorothy's mother, but someone's mother, or someone's idea of one. It was the voice of her therapist. Her first one. Not her second one. Her second therapist was not accepting.

"Sometimes it takes longer than ten days," the doctor added.

The doctor was a human like any other, like Dorothy herself. She could not repair everything that was broken. Her voice and its unanxious capaciousness indicated to Dorothy that the relationship of the average to the individual was mysterious and balanced; to arrive at an average bleed of ten days some people had to bleed much longer. By exceeding the average, Dorothy's life was intimately connected to it. By bleeding more than average Dorothy was making it possible for others to bleed less.

Voices from the nurses' desk filtered into the room: who was doing what this weekend, who needed to "leave a sample." A burst of laughter. Inside the exam room the light was harsh. A framed reproduction on the wall featured a large pregnant woman in a blue tunic holding her potato-shaped head like she was about to pull it off her neck. There was a hole in the middle of her shirt that revealed a purple fetus. The fetus floated head up, in breech. Poor upright baby, born of headless woman!

"Should I have gotten the in-office procedure?" Dorothy asked. "The vacuum?"

"If this were to happen again we would recommend it," said the doctor, and Dorothy marveled at the delicacy with which she pronounced that "if." There was no hint of probability, no whiff of omen, no blame. Where did people learn to speak this way, in flat neutral statements? "You're a bleeder."

In one sense there was nothing in there. A little snow. Some dust, really. Some uterus dust that needed a good sweeping.

But it wouldn't be right to call it empty. Empty indicated something clean and hard and final. It looked like a black hole on the screen but Dorothy knew enough to know that the density was sponge; it was soft in there, things got stuck.

The shape on the screen, the shadow, was undeniably Dorothy's. The wand was inside her and no one else, the sound waves could be bouncing around nothing except her interior walls. And yet the picture felt distant, like the wand was a radio receiving signals from deep space or deep underwater rather than from herself. She was too shallow to have an interior this deep. She felt like an observer of some other reality, looking not into a mirror but through a portal or at the page of an old illustrated book. It was hard to read; it was like a map she couldn't orient herself to or a medieval manuscript, and she needed someone else to explain what it had to do with her. It was nothing like her favorite scene in *The Magic Mountain,* of Hans Castorp having his X-ray taken:

> *And Hans Castorp saw exactly what he should have expected to see, but which no man was ever intended to see and which he himself had never presumed he would be able to see: he saw his own grave. Under that light, he saw the process of corruption anticipated, saw the flesh in which he moved decomposed, expunged, dissolved into airy nothingness—and inside was the delicately turned skeleton of his right hand and around the last joint of the ring finger, dangling black and loose, the signet ring his grandfather had bequeathed him: a hard thing, this ore with which man adorns a body predestined to melt away beneath it, so that it can be free again and move on to yet other flesh that may bear it for a while. With the eyes of his Tienappel forebear—penetrating, clairvoyant eyes—he beheld a familiar part of his body, and for the first time in his life he understood that he would die. And he made the same face he usually made when listening to music—a rather dull, sleepy, and devout face, his head tilted toward one shoulder, his mouth half-open.*

Dorothy did not feel, eyeing the onscreen uterus, vacant of all but a few reluctant bloodstrings, that she was looking at her own death, or a premonition of her death, but something more like a foreclosure—an abandoned or evacuated property. Someone had left in a hurry, a criminal or a deviant person, who had not taken the time to properly clean up after herself. It was a scene roped off with yellow tape, shot by a security camera for an episode of crime television. Of course, Hans Castorp had been looking at bones, so maybe that explained the gravity of his feelings, the concreteness of his epiphany, his sense that he was meeting his own future self. His confrontation was with the very structure of the, his, human form, and with, no less, the hand—the part of the body that reaches out, that is manipulative, active, external, that writes and drives and builds and prays and feeds. The hand. Dorothy was looking at a spongy interior, a disused room, a warehouse for a shell company, a cavern or cave. She knew from her undergraduate education that the shadows projected on the walls of a cave are never to be trusted, that they lack the reality of flesh, and of philosophy. If the womb was a grave it was also a junk drawer. How strange, too, that these images of herself, and the images of the unborn that she had seen on signs growing up, that she herself had glued onto posterboard and reinforced with cardboard, were drawn by sounds. The sounds hit some resistance, some boundary between densities, and bounced back in image. They were echoes that had faces. Hans Castorp had not had to reckon with that synesthetic paradox.

She had chanted while they carried the sound pictures, the aural images, her exuberant preteen voice merging in festival with the grown-ups around her: *It's a child, not a choice.* Dorothy had never understood how the same women who were vociferous defenders of abortion rights could festoon their refrigerators and social media feeds with fetal photography. It must be that other people were more secure in their power to declare when and whether a life was a human. If you wanted it, it was a baby and you could email it around to your friends; if you didn't, it was an act of violence to be asked to look at it. Dorothy basically agreed with this position or believed that people had the right to have this position but she couldn't summon the will to assume it herself. It wasn't that it was incoherent so much as it was overconfident. And what about the joy with which women greet their pregnancies? Was that protesting too much? Didn't everyone feel that it was basically disgusting, the way that a parasite burrows inside you, quietly making you ill while it goes about acquiring a soul and the legal status of a human? What kind of loss was it for one of these creatures to fail to progress, and what was the appropriate feeling to have in response?

It awed her, not only the doctor's proximity to this technology, but the casual way she manipulated the probe and the screen. The doctor had a deep knowledge of the machine's ways, a practiced ease of handling; she seemed not overly impressed by her power to freeze motion, to turn sound into sight. Unlike a priest overseeing a rite, she had no deep respect or hesitation at the foot of the almighty.

"I'd like a printout," Dorothy heard herself saying. "A photo."

The doctor turned to her too quickly to mask the surprise on her petaled face.

"We don't usually do that," she said, "in situations like these."

Dorothy hated to disappoint her but could not give in.

"This might be my only chance for a sonogram of myself," she said. "Is it an insurance thing? What does it cost?"

The doctor looked sad, like she had expected more of Dorothy—expected her to act in accordance with whatever norms this situation contained. To be disappointed but not grieving, to be interested but not morbid. To understand her situation as a medical event, and not to ask for a souvenir.

But without another word—without a word about expense, or insurance, or taste, or decorum—she tapped some buttons and the computer spat out one grainy dark photo.

"Thank you," said Dorothy.

The wand slid out and Dorothy relaxed. The doctor flipped the lights back on and Dorothy scooted her hips off the end of the chair. She pushed up from the forced recumbent position.

"Call if you have any questions," the doctor said, and shut the door.

Alone, Dorothy studied the glossy square of paper. Frozen, it lacked the mystery of the moving image; the trails were dead pixels, was all. She cleaned the translucent goop from her vagina as best she could and threw the wad of tissues in the open trash can; thinking better of it, she lifted them up with a finger and stuffed them into the biohazard can. She dressed and left the room quickly, though not before folding the purple cotton robe. In the waiting room Dorothy felt the eyes of the other patients longing to congratulate her. On the street she joined the crowd, where each one of the people she saw and all the people she didn't see, the ones scuttling through the buildings above and burrowed on the rails underground, had grown—been grown—inside of a mother. All of these people, every one, they all had begun as a pulsing circle that, within days, sprouted limbs, and later, intentions. They had all been inside the inflatable petri dish of the mother and they had all gotten out. In doing so, all had caused their mothers pain. All had caused their mothers bleeding. Some had nearly killed their mothers. Yet here they were, walking around in their confusion of attire, unsure how to dress for the temperatures that rose and fell without warning, engaged in pursuits noble and unredeemed, these grown-up emergency cesareans, these prolapsed uteruses, these givers of preeclampsia who had, most of them, and remarkably autonomously, all things considered, acquired mobility, language, and the ability to perceive what sensations came from inside their bodies and which were the province of the outside.

When Dorothy was ripp'd untimely from her mother's womb, the anesthesiologist had given her mother such a heavy dose of sedative that mother and daughter had not met until half a day later. Dorothy didn't know who had held her in those hours while her mother was sedated. Maybe a nurse did. Maybe no one. In those days it was not thought so essential to hold a newborn.

"Watch where you're going, bitch," a head attached to a pair of legs sprawled across the sidewalk said. Dorothy apologized and redirected her attention to avoiding the obstacles of the street, keeping one hand buried in her bag, gripping the leather wallet where the evidence of her watery insides was creased between dollar bills and ancient ATM receipts.

That night Dorothy put on her nice black pants and went downtown to meet her mother and Rachel for the underwater puppet show. If anyone other than Dorothy's mother had invited her to an underwater puppet show, she would have thought it was a joke. In a way it was. Not the invitation itself, but its presentation. "I want to have a cultural evening with both my daughters," her mother had said on the phone. That was the joke: "both my daughters."

Rachel was her mother's mentee, or surrogate daughter, or friend; Dorothy was never quite sure how to refer to her, even in her own mind. Rachel was a junior in high school. She had parents of her own, but there had been conflict at home over Rachel's boyfriend, who was twenty-three and a student at the local community college, as well as other rebellions, and Dorothy's mother, who knew Rachel from the neighborhood, where they both walked the same breed of terrier early in the morning, had become her mentor, or surrogate parent, or confidante. She took Rachel to the movies, the mall; they talked on the phone. Had Dorothy herself entertained the affections of a grown man when she had been a teen, her mother would not have been nearly so forgiving; age or distance had mellowed her, and Dorothy supposed she ought to respect her mother's growth, although she couldn't help but feel jealous that Rachel received the kind of relaxed acceptance that Dorothy had been denied. Her first therapist had theorized that her mother liked Rachel because it was a way not only of rewriting the kind of mother she had been to Dorothy, but also of extending her maternal temporality. If her mother ever felt that Dorothy growing up and swimming away meant that she herself was old, she didn't have to feel that way with Rachel. Dorothy was old and had made mistakes and had turned out a certain way, which meant she had not turned out other ways, but Rachel was young and her most meaningful mistakes were still ahead of her; when Rachel got old, Dorothy's mother could get a new Rachel, which is to say, a new new Dorothy.

As a theory it sounded plausible to Dorothy, though it also suggested that the cycle of surrogacy could go on forever, in the way that people use pets. Where children are always changing, demanding change, where their bodies are clocks marking the passage of years, pet ownership stops time, allowing a person to dwell permanently in the same routine. As soon as a pet is housebroken they have learned all they will ever learn; they are on a course of absolute stasis. Thus, Dorothy reasoned, the trauma when a pet dies—not only has the owner lost companionship, but time itself has ruptured or split open.

Dorothy didn't like where her mind was going—did she really think a pet dying would be more disruptive than the death of a human child?—but the point, she thought, was that Rachel was her mother's pet, and allowed her mother an existential recursion. Everyone had their way of denying linearity. Men left their wives for younger women; women acquired mentees. If you wanted to fool yourself that something wasn't ending, you just had to go out and start something that was pretty much the same. This hurt, of course, the feeling of being replaced or replaceable, the sense that one daughter was not enough for her mother. Not that her mother saw it that way. Her mother told her repeatedly how much she loved her, that she would love her no matter who she was or what she did, though such assurances hardly helped. Love, Dorothy believed, should be unconditional in the sense that one is so intrinsically and beautifully worthwhile that no crimes or foibles or stupidity can diminish one's essential attractiveness, sympathy, and worth, but conditional insofar as it depends on one's unique appeal. The problem with parents was that the love they offered, while necessary, was ultimately tautological. They loved their children because they were their children; they would have loved whoever they got, which meant that it did not matter who you were. Dorothy's mother once said that the purpose of motherhood was to teach your child how to love other people, to show them the right way to leave you, which sounded noble, although the presence of Rachel indicated that mothers could not live on nobility alone.

The three women and their tiny paper cups of espresso squeezed onto a red velvet couch and waited for the ushers to let them downstairs. "I was asking about your day?" her mother said. "Did you have a productive day?"

Dorothy's mother had told her so many times that she was not disappointed by Dorothy that Dorothy had to assume her mother was very disappointed, or at least deeply ambivalent, and could express it only through disavowal. Her mother had told her so many times that she would have loved her the same if she had been a garbageman that Dorothy could only conclude that her mother would have preferred that profession for her, or perhaps that academia and sanitation were, in her mother's mind, somehow equivalent. Alas, while sanitation workers disposed of trash, performing an essential and worthy civic function, all Dorothy did was move it from one pile to another.

"Also," her mother said, "you have something in your teeth."

Dorothy picked at two wrong places and dug fruitlessly in the right place until she took her phone out to use it as a mirror.

"You got it," said her mother and Rachel at the same time, and laughed.

Because the blood was dawdling its way so slowly out of her

vagina, because it wasn't something she felt until it was already half-dry, because actually there was so little blood at this point that she didn't even feel it on the liner, and only knew she was bleeding because she wiped it out with toilet paper—for all these reasons it wasn't a lie, when her mother looked at her with strange, half-illuminated worry, and asked how she was feeling, that Dorothy didn't acknowledge anything below the waist.

"My shoulder hurts," she said truthfully. "Also my wrists. From the computer."

"Do you have tingling in the fingertips?" her mother asked. "I get that from my phone."

"It's more of a stinging sensation in my cuticle," Dorothy said. "But just this one."

She held up her right hand and rubbed the side pad of the ring finger.

"It throbs a little and when I push on it, it's sore," Dorothy said, demonstrating. "Also, shooting pains in my forearms."

Rachel, who played the double bass and knew about repetitive stress, asked if Dorothy had an injury.

"It's called the twenty-first century," Dorothy said, and her mother rolled her eyes.

"Is that a joke?" asked Rachel, and then it was time to go into the theater.

Earlier that day Dorothy had taken her mother's advice and read up on the postshow backstage tour, which was optional but which no one in their right mind would skip, and served as an informal epilogue to the performance. The "puppets" were abstractions, not characters, consisting of ribbons of fabric and other items readily available in craft stores, like scarves and pom-poms. On the tour, audience members would discover that the puppeteers wore wetsuits, that they were extremely strong and acrobatic, that some of them worked suspended from wires and cables and actually flew over the aquarium tank, dipping and gliding their tools. (Others of them reached into the tank from a raised platform.) The show, which had debuted decades earlier—this was a reprisal—was the brainchild of a young and bold third-generation puppeteer who had gone on to a celebrated career in more traditionally narrative puppeteering. In a program note, he compared himself to Kandinsky. The show, the same review explained, had no plot; it was pure color and light, something like an animated painting or canvas, and it was performed to a live accompaniment of Berlioz's *Symphonie Fantastique,* which also gave the show its name—*Symphonie Fantastique.*

Rachel, it turned out, had recently learned this very Berlioz piece, *Symphonie Fantastique,* in the youth orchestra in which she played double bass, and had somehow, through her precocious perusal of the arts listings, or the advice of the director of the orchestra, learned of the run. While tardier ticket-holders filed into the rows behind them, Rachel, who had grown several inches since the last time Dorothy had seen her, and whose face was expertly highlighted and shadowed with products whose names Dorothy could not even guess at, explained that her favorite movement of the piece was the fourth one, where the artist, who throughout the symphony is on a kind of romantic quest, has an opium dream in which he witnesses his own execution.

"It's the *fatal blow,*" Rachel said, and Dorothy felt sure she was quoting.

She felt sure, too, that Rachel, despite her attempts to manufacture sophistication, and her expertise at illuminating her face, was too young to know anything of the horror of what she was saying, that to her, "the fatal blow" was an empty, glittery bit of vocabulary, flying around in the air, that she could grab with her calloused fingers and sprinkle around her persona for decoration, whereas Dorothy, despite not having witnessed her own execution, had suffered other failures, the twisted-metal catastrophe of real life. Dorothy was at the age where choices revealed themselves as errors, increasingly acquiring the patina of irrevocability. For Rachel, life's tragedies still had a premature, anticipated quality; they were romantic. She looked to the future, careering along toward a glorious climax of love or death. Rachel didn't understand the small, bureaucratic, quotidian, present tense. Dorothy did not mind her mother adopting Rachel, or Rachel adopting her mother, did not mind Rachel tagging along or even tagging along with Rachel, whichever way it was, but listening to Rachel prattle on about Berlioz, and lower her voice at the word "opium," as if it were the *scandale* of the season, that was a bridge too far, sororally speaking.

An older couple, their teenage son, and his shopping bag settled directly behind Dorothy's party. After they had removed their jackets and argued about where to put the shopping bag—the boy wanted to give it its own seat, but the father insisted it go on the floor, and finally the mother consented to put it on her lap—they commenced to argue about where to eat dinner, and what time the last train left the station.

"Oh, he took *opium*," said the woman, who must have been leafing through the program notes.

"He had a dream," said Rachel, turning around. "He saw his own execution."

"Did he!" said the other mother.

"Is she yours?" said the other mother. "She's very smart."

"They're both with me," Dorothy's mother said.

"Why don't you tell her that I'm your real daughter?" Dorothy whispered.

"Dorothy!" her mother tsked. "I don't need strangers knowing our business," she added softly, and for once, Dorothy agreed.

An "underwater puppet show" was not the kind of thing Dorothy would normally attend, because, she acknowledged silently to herself as she sat in the front row, spellbound and in a heightened state of sensory receptivity, she was a snob, and worse—fearful and fundamentally closed off to new experiences. In matters of aesthetics she was a philistine, a slave to bourgeois narrative conventions. She had believed characters mattered, events. Chasing the little slips of ribbon and paper with her gaze, Dorothy chastised herself for having expected *Symphonie Fantastique* to build to some kind of crescendo, to increase in drama, to achieve a frenzy or orgiastic fever of choreography, color, texture—something. She had not consciously anticipated the build. But she experienced the absence of build, the unmet expectation. While the music came to at least one climax, just as Rachel had explained it would, the visual performance, resplendent with sparkles and arabesqueing handkerchiefs, offered instead, from act to act, a dreamy stasis. Even as the melody built or retreated, telling a story that culminated, according to Rachel, in a witches' dance, the fabrics swirled and popped, disappeared and scattered, with a rhythmic eddy that mimed the music's beats but whose overall effect was at once stimulating and soothing and that never fundamentally increased in intensity. It rose and fell but the peaks and valleys were within a compressed range. There was nowhere to get to, Dorothy realized at a certain point, and half-expected the show to suddenly end with her epiphany; instead, the show went on. The work had no relation to her ideas about it, or rather, her ideas were free to come and go as they pleased, just as these glorified bits of seagrass, made out of—was it construction paper? Waterproof construction paper?—came and went. This was art without progress, a succession of images, immersing its audience in an ongoing present. It didn't matter if Dorothy remembered what came before or if she was prepared for what came next, there was nothing to prepare for. This wasn't to say that the performance did not contain surprises, only that the experience was constant surprise, which she experienced not as interruption but as rolling transformation.

She felt herself in a lucid dream, where she could control the puppets with her mind. They did exactly what she wanted them to do, or perhaps whatever they did turned out to be the answer to hitherto unknown desires that came into being only in the instant of their satisfaction; she was totally gratified and also falling asleep. She sat up straighter, not because it would be rude to fall asleep—she felt, on the contrary, that it would be the highest compliment one could pay to such a fantasia— but because she did not want Rachel to think she was bored. Ego battled languor, a state that superficially resembled boredom but was in fact evidence of absolute satiation, even bliss.

In the space between the pianist's notes she could hear the boy behind her breathing. His breaths turned into snores— gentle, choking sounds, like someone inhaling through a mask.

The pianist had the kind of curly hair that is caused by electrical shock. He was a replacement pianist. The real pianist was sick.

Of course, this guy was real, too. Just look at him. His arms pumped up and down like he was shoveling the notes up out of the ground.

It was odd, she thought now, soothed/hypnotized by a screen saver come to life and hydrated, how she didn't even know what verb to use to describe the movement of blood out of her vagina. It wasn't coursing. It wasn't draining. It wasn't flowing or seeping. It was like paint on an old house that occasionally peeled off in a slab. It flaked out of her. Or trickled, like the syrup too stubborn to come down from the inside of a jar after being upside down for days and fucking days.

A bright yellow curtain pleated and accordioned in and out

in the water, imitating bellows, or lungs breathing. Or it wasn't imitating anything, it was just itself, a meditation on—pleats. Dorothy hadn't known that pleats stayed in fabric when it got wet. Maybe not if it got too wet? She didn't understand how they got pleats into fabric or what made them disappear or how you ironed them back in if they disappeared. Dorothy refused to fault herself for being unable to perform the most basic domestic tasks. She was the achievement of feminism. When buttons fell off her clothes, she paid the dry cleaner to sew them back on. But if this was victory, why did it feel like defeat?

But now, Dorothy wondered: What was failure? What was success? Ribbons swirling in a cold tank. Life was not a story that ended on a resolution or a revelation. It was like this puppet show—a gentle, ongoing state of ups and downs that contained moments of illusory transcendence and ultimately built to nothing, no epiphanies, or so many epiphanies that they ran together and were forgotten. Maybe it breathed like a paper flower, expanding and contracting. Maybe it was something you did just to pass the time.

Eventually the puppet show ended, with the same lack of fanfare with which it began, but it ended. At this moment and only this moment did it concede to convention. It spoke the universal language of endings: The curtain came down, the lights came up. One world receded and yielded to another. Dorothy said, as they waited on line for the backstage tour, that she could have watched it for twice as long and, conversely, would have been happy with it being half its length. Rachel claimed to have been riveted the entire time, though she admitted that the snoring that came from the row behind them had been a distraction. Dorothy's mother was fresh and awake. She had silently power-napped through the whole last movement.

"I got the idea," she said. "I don't feel like I missed anything."

That night there was bright red blood on the toilet paper. Rog had started buying the brown recycled toilet paper, which Dorothy didn't really believe would make the world better but at least wouldn't make it worse, and the bloodstain looked like fall, like one veiny, vibrant leaf on a tree. Was she a tree? Or was her body a slot machine randomly ejecting globs of blood? It was a feature, not a bug. She stuck her finger all the way inside and pulled it out again. Nothing. She sniffed it. She walked into the bedroom pantsless and turned on the fan. She dug around in her bag and wallet and pulled out the photo from the morning and studied it in the yellow glow of the lamp. She wished there was someplace she could put her body down for a while, just a little while, before getting back into it.

Without warning, in the grim hotel bathroom, the toilet paper returned a large brown lump. Cable news was blaring from the television. From inside the bathroom the pundits sounded less like invited company and more like forced entrants. It had been three weeks at least since the bleeding had stopped, but now that stop had to be called an interruption, the last bleed no longer the last, but the last until now. But was it really bleeding? Leaving aside the issue of tissue vs. blood, even if she was using "bleeding" to indicate any emission, this bleeding was more like a delivery that had been lost in the mail, like starlight, a dead message from the past. Dorothy's pants were bunched below her knees. The professor in her was pleased that her menstrual vocabulary, previously limited to terms such as "light," "heavy," and "spotting," was expanding. Again photography had been proven to be a distortion of reality. This mass wasn't at all what the sonogram had forecast. It was clotted, not tendrily. She contemplated an Internet search, but knew it would only return information that would be terrifying and irrelevant, and anyway, the doctor had told her not to worry. She tried to pull the lump apart with her fingers; it was like resin, sticky and congealed, and she felt a stab of guilt for trying to take apart what so clearly wanted to be whole.

On the plane yesterday everyone had been drinking and carousing, like they were in a commercial for Las Vegas, and Dorothy was in the commercial, too, cast as the slightly sour, stick-in-the-mud friend who would have to be cajoled into having a good time but who, by the time the city and all its seductions had gotten into her, would never want to go home. The plan had been to use the flying time to get work done, so while the people around her downed miniature bottles of spirits, Dorothy put in her earplugs and opened a much-annotated copy of *The Way of the World.* She had been anticipating returning to this text as one anticipates a reunion with an old friend with whom one is not in regular touch—with a mixture of forced enthusiasm and hesitation, the insistence that it's so great to see you doing battle with the shared conviction that one would really rather not. She found her page, and almost immediately the book began to speak.

Look at me! the book said.

What? said Dorothy, underlining a sentence about how *Middlemarch* is the only nineteenth-century English novel "which dares to deal with the major theme of the European *Bildungsroman:* failure."

I have read all of Stendhal in French, the book informed her nonchalantly. Dorothy nodded and proceeded to the useless labor of underlining the phrases "objective historical demands" and "significant for novelistic narration," both of which were already italicized. *I understand the internal logic of formal contradictions,* the book added, straining to be heard over the chatter in the rows behind. *Tell me again what you do?*

That's not my field, Dorothy started to say, but the book talked over her.

Greater minds than yours, it said, *minds more serious, more synthetic, with better recall, more command of foreign languages—and actual political commitments, by the way, which you, for reasons relating to your own disappointed cynicism, hatred of groups, and existential damage that manifests as useless contrarianism and resignation, can't bear to make—have toiled and turned this loamy field.*

Loamy? said Dorothy.

It means fertile, said the book.

I know, Dorothy said, flipping back to the pages about fairy tales. *Your work is superfluous,* her unpleasant companion went on, *but far from being superfluous in the lovely, decorative sense of a sweet, impermanent trifle that will bring delight and assuage the sufferings of others, like birdsong, your superfluity is a ghastly excess.*

Dorothy opened the air vent above. The book raised its voice, shouting through the creases in its wrinkled spine. *You,* it exclaimed, pausing to clear a frog of phlegm from its throat, *are a dilettante, a prosaic clog in the pipes of discourse. The problem of the twenty-first century is a problem of waste!* She closed the book, but the blurbs taunted her. *Don't you know anything, you joke of a humanist, you walking fatberg of consumer debt?*

The flight attendant was leaning over her, trying to give her peanuts. She took the peanuts. She lowered her tray table and suffocated the muttering book between her leg and the armrest and selected from the in-flight entertainment system a movie about undercover police officers infiltrating a high school. The officers were on the trail of a potent new drug. One of the officers was short and fat and one was conventionally handsome, but according to millennial logic, it was the nerd who was cool and the suave jock was passé. Dorothy was in the aisle seat, using a big sweater as a blanket. The man in the middle was highlighting passages in a book about blackjack strategy. The person in the window seat had thrown an airline blanket over their face and was sleeping or pretending to sleep. When the movie ended Dorothy started it again, without bothering to research the other entertainment options. She did that not because she was in a state of depressed indifference or ennui but because she had genuinely enjoyed the movie, and didn't want it to end.

The taxi ride from the airport was confusing. Dorothy did

not feel capable of processing the landmarks. It was her first time in Las Vegas. She hugged her bag and kept saying to herself, *I'm in Las Vegas,* as if that would help.

After depositing her luggage in a small, dim room in the upper heavens of Harrah's, she went for a walk on the Strip. The number of young children was a surprise. Everyone was drinking through twisty straws. All ages. It was like Disney World, except there were no animals and no rides and when you thought about the mass transfer of capital from individual Social Security accounts into casino coffers you wanted to stab yourself with a twisty straw. The crowd meandered, stopping frequently to gawk or take photographs of signs or themselves, but Dorothy, trained to walk purposefully on New York streets, moved with precision, finding the undefended pockets of space as skillfully as any professional athlete. It was ninety-two degrees and the sweat pooled behind her knees and gathered at her brow. The back of her neck, under her hair, was sweaty. The casinos were so big that there was no one place to stand that offered a satisfactory experience of seeing them in their totality; being across the street helped, but only a little. They had impressive architectural entryways, large mouths that wanted to swallow you and you let them do it because it was cool inside. She crossed the street to be closer to the jumping fountains outside the Bellagio. Presumably the water was recycled and recirculated but it still seemed, in its ostentation, a gross celebration from simpler, happier times. The fountain said, *Don't worry about resources.* It said, *There is enough for everyone and more for the show.* That was all it said. She liked watching it.

She made it as far as Paris before turning back, panting and thirsty, for the opening reception of the conference, where conversation revolved around the conference organizers' choice of first, Vegas, and second, Harrah's. On the edge of the group she saw Keith, an—acquaintance? Friend? Ex?—from grad school, who had gone on to a tenure-track job at Johns Hopkins. Keith was more handsome than she remembered—grayer and leaner, like he had taken up a fitness regime. He wore red threads around his wrists. He was glad to see her. His eyes latched on to Dorothy's with barbed hooks. His hand grabbed her hand, his mouth kissed her cheek. Dorothy tried to remember when she had agreed that any man who felt like it was permitted to put his open mouth on her face. It didn't make her angry that men did this, she just wanted to know when she had signed off on it.

She used to think a lot about how different her life would be if she had wound up with Keith—in an idle way, not as a real counterfactual. It would never have worked out. It didn't work out. Keith was rich, which Dorothy had liked, but stingy, which she didn't. He always wanted to split the bill. Their thing lasted only a couple months. It might have gone on forever except one weekend he brought her to his little cabin in the country, where, instead of having sex and letting her fall asleep with her face in his armpit, which smelled amazing, he announced that he wanted to "try something." This something turned out to be whispering into her vagina for almost an hour while she shivered beneath a thin flannel blanket and occasionally remembered to pet his head. Poems by Frank O'Hara. He whispered poems by Frank O'Hara into her vagina.

He did stuff with his tongue, too, but it was all timed to the poems and Dorothy lay there under the single Edison bulb with its lightning rod of golden filament crackling, wondering how, when, where he got the idea that this was a good idea. Was she the guinea pig? Or was this tried and true? Had this been somebody's favorite thing? He wasn't talking *to* her vagina, it wasn't like he had original content he needed to communicate to it; it wasn't like she, Dorothy, was being addressed. She had been confused for somebody else, the kind of person who could orgasm over a poem. Or was the idea that you could say anything into any vagina and the vibrations of air would have their effect? In that case, why poems? Dorothy didn't even like poems. How had Keith gotten the idea that she did? Did she seem like a poem person? What was wrong with how she was presenting herself to the world that this kind of misrecognition was even possible?

"I thought you loved language" was what he said when he finally gave up. A good sport, he reached down with his hand, but Dorothy pushed him away as politely as she could.

"Wow" was what she said.

What she most remembered about this unpleasant night was Keith's face, which he periodically withdrew to assess his progress and announce each subsequent title, like he was giving a reading, like he had written these poems himself. It was so eager and proud, like a dog's after it brings some disgusting prize to its owner. Remembering it now, Dorothy recoiled with shame. What was wrong with the way they had done things before, that was what Dorothy still could not understand. Life was hard enough without taking easy victories away. But Keith, it seemed, had been bored by her, or he hated her, or, most disturbingly, their ideas of pleasure were so different that his way of expressing affection was perceived by Dorothy as an affront bordering on an offense. The next week she met Rog and a couple weeks after that Keith got together with a pint-size art historian and when they saw each other in seminar he acted like everything was totally normal, they were just two overeducated chimpanzees who used to take off their pants and whisper into each other's genitals in Connecticut and now were content comparing notes on Franco Moretti.

What she had shared and done with Keith—even if she hadn't done it herself, she had been there, she was implicated—was, Dorothy knew, more intimate than anything she had ever done or shared with Rog. But intimacy wasn't in itself a good thing. There was such a thing as privacy. Rog would never impinge on her the way Keith had, would never expose her. Through disinterest or tenderness he permitted her to remain intact, a little hidden from him. He always showed her exquisite courtesy.

"Did you hear," said Keith, leaning close in a way that suggested drunkenness, "about Elyse?" Dorothy knew Elyse slightly from a Texas conference two years prior where they had presented on the same panel. Elyse's research was about the history of meteorological reports; she had a theory about how practices in weather observation had impacted the development of literary description. It was a clever idea, and timely, and Dorothy had enjoyed Elyse's paper. Usually Dorothy was jealous of what she enjoyed, but on that occasion she was aware that she did not wish Elyse's research was her own. Elyse's conclusions were interesting, but arriving at them seemed boring; Dorothy had no appetite for data. She would never call her work "research."

In addition to her scholarly virtues, Elyse was widely acknowledged as sexy, rather in the way of an artist or elementary school teacher; she always looked a little sloppy, she carried around some aura of bedsheets and papier-mâché. Her eyebrows were dark and unruly and she never wore the typical female academic uniform of black blazer enlivened with large pendant or "statement necklace"; she favored slouchy overalls, interesting collars, dramatic patterns, and large hoop earrings. It was like she was dressing for a different life, or had a different life, off this stage and on some other. She had been married the last time Dorothy had seen her, but, according to Keith, in the intervening period Elyse had gotten a divorce. He tottered back and wiped saliva from the corner of his mouth. It was no surprise that Keith desired Elyse or that he was friends with her. Elyse and Keith had done the same postdoc and friendship blossomed between them as easily as professional laurels were exchanged; after the Texas panel, in fact, Keith had solicited Elyse to contribute to a journal issue he was editing, an issue celebrating the work of the scholar Lauren Berlant and her theory of "cruel optimism."

"Cruel optimism" was Berlant's way of theorizing why and how people remained attached to fantasies and aspirations of "the good life," how those aspirations injured them, and the resulting affect—something she called "stuckness." "Cruel optimism" was Dorothy's entire life. But Keith had not solicited a contribution from Dorothy. He had, instead, emailed her to explain that this lack of invitation was not a sign of disrespect but the contrary—he respected her so much that he did not want to burden her when he knew, as all of Dorothy's circle knew, that she was behind on her manuscript, her only chance of escaping, as he put it, "adjunct hell." In other words, Dorothy knew too much about cruel optimism to write about it. When the journal arrived, she put it on the dresser/nightstand on top of the other books and magazines she intended to read. After months of not reading, she moved it to the coffee table, where it lingered until Rog, in a rare burst of tidying fever, moved it to the pile of catalogs and boxes by the recycling bag and then, some weeks later, after Dorothy informed him that she had every intention of devoting herself to its contents, back to the dresser/nightstand, where it currently resided, facedown, under a coaster.

Dorothy said she was sorry to hear about Elyse's divorce. Keith shrugged.

"We're in the lull between first weddings and second weddings," he said. "The parties for the second weddings won't be as good, but we'll be older, so we'll appreciate them more."

The consensus among the young professors at the mixer was that while it was fun in a "try anything once" way to be in Vegas, Harrah's was gross. They wanted to be at the Wynn, or New York–New York.

"I like Harrah's," said Keith, but he was only being contrarian—or ironic, Dorothy wasn't sure. Being around Keith usually didn't bother Dorothy, in fact she liked him as a person and respected his intellect, but tonight he made her feel like she was molding. Was that what you called it when you turned into mold? Or did that imply she was turning into a cornice? She resented being forced to think this way. She didn't want the memory; she wanted to give it back. She said something about needing to finish her paper and excused herself. No one begged her to stay.

Harrah's permitted indoor smoking but had not installed a ventilation system, so when Dorothy wandered the aisles of slot machines, as she did before going up to her room for the night, she covered her mouth with her hand and breathed in her own recirculated air, shivering. She fell asleep hungry, because she had eaten all her granola bars on the plane. Four hours later she woke in all her clothes, her contact lenses cracking in her eyes, and stumbled to the bathroom to pry them out with unwashed fingers.

That was yesterday. Now it was today. Her panel had begun early, promptly at nine A.M., in a well-refrigerated ballroom. The other panelists were strangers to her but she noticed, during the second paper (she was last), all the way in the back of the room, a woman with huge, inquisitive eyes, gripping the back of her neck in furious concentration. It was Elyse.

The quiet of the ballroom was broken by the occasional shifting or rummaging through a bag, but it was otherwise very silent; even the cooling system, which was working to maximum effect, was silent. The second panelist leaned in close to the microphone and heavily aspirated his *p*'s and *t*'s. Dorothy had listened keenly to the first panelist, whose paper was on shadows, but the second panelist, who droned on through long thickets of quotation, was harder to follow. Was this how people felt about her work? Elyse must have been trying to catch Dorothy's eye for some time because as soon as Dorothy allowed her gaze to drift over the sparsely filled seats—there was a more exciting panel taking place several ballrooms down, not the keynote but a panel of big, contentious personalities, who attract conference-goers like a fireplace attracts weary travelers, or flies descend, convivially, on a dumpster—Elyse pointed frantically at her watch, made a sad face, pointed to the exit, tapped herself repeatedly on the shoulder, waved a sheaf of papers in the air, danced a finger over them, and shrugged, a series of honey-bee imitations that communicated—what, Dorothy was not sure. If Elyse had her own paper to give, she would have already been up on a dais somewhere; if she wanted to attend the more exciting panel of noted personalities, why wasn't she there? Satisfied that she had been understood, Elyse pulled on a shapeless white coat (even across the room it muted her complexion, somewhat diminishing her beauty), made a "hang ten" gesture, and put her hand to her ear like a receiver and then corrected herself by thumbing an imaginary phone, indicating that she would text Dorothy later, which she did, first apologizing, then explaining—an explanation that morphed seamlessly into a boast—that she had run off to finish writing her own paper, which departed from her previous interest in clouds to explore her new interest, botany, and had gone over better than she ever could have imagined. Then she suggested that they meet for dinner that night. Dorothy wrote back, "Sounds good!"

After the panel Dorothy went to her room and took off her uncomfortable booties. Odd how her fanciest shoes, which she wore only when she needed to seem mature or command respect, were also the ones with the most infantile name. She knew she ought to be attending the other panels, where, if she were smart, she would distinguish herself by asking pointed and memorable questions, questions that, if they were pointed and memorable enough, might lead to being deemed by her peers to be a significant voice, or even, if her questions led to conversations that led to invitations to contribute to journals, appear on other panels, give lectures, etc., her redemption from the limbo of contingency—a phrase she preferred to "adjunct hell," which at once overstated and understated (by glossing over) her position—but she had an appointment to keep.

Was it time? It was almost time.

She opened her laptop, promised the system prompt that she would attend to it tomorrow, removed the electrical tape that usually covered the camera lens, opened Photo Booth, and checked how she appeared onscreen. The lighting in the room was dim, which made her face appear yellow and mottled with shadows; when she turned the light brighter, her face brightened into a sickly gray. She tilted the screen down-up-down again. She opened the heavy curtains but the sky was overcast and the pale imitation of sunshine drained the effectiveness of the electrical light rather than enhancing it. She closed the heavy curtains again and tried to enjoy a reprieve from diurnal time, but it was too depressing; she finally settled on opening the heavy curtains but leaving the white scrim closed.

Her face looked artificial, stricken. She seemed to have a moustache. She knew it was the shadow cast by her large nose over the divot in her lip but that didn't change the fact that it appeared to be a moustache. There wasn't time to fix the situation, or rather, time wouldn't be the thing that fixed it. She went to the bathroom, where she expelled the brown lump.

The lump, as stated, was resiny.

"Resin" always made Dorothy think of the year she had taken violin lessons. She had hated playing the violin. Her arm wasn't strong enough to hold it up. She never advanced past "Twinkle, Twinkle, Little Star."

It could be a clot but Dorothy had a feeling it was fetal material. Like how an egg was a deconstructed—preconstructed—chicken. If everything had been different these matted-together cells could have been molded into kidneys, lungs, cartilage, all the stuff. The nails. The gray matter of the brain.

When exactly did the fetus pass into humanity? It was a question on which people could not agree. It involved a gory transition, things that were slippery and malformed. Dorothy was afraid of fetuses. They were creatures from a horror movie. If you saw one lying on the bed you would run from the room screaming. But maybe you wouldn't. Maybe your maternal feelings would be so strong that you would tenderly wrap your fetus in a blanket and press its frog-like mouth to your breast. Dorothy's heart raced. She longed to encounter the abominable horror of creation, to test herself against its power. But she was no mad scientist, no Victor Frankenstein. No hands or feet had come stillborn out of her. It was not that extreme. Hers was a situation, not a trauma. A trauma implied an event, a shock, before and after. The situation persisted; it ground away, day by day, with an ordinary, odorous, calendrical drip. It was tissue, all the way down.

The light in the bathroom reminded Dorothy of the department-store dressing rooms her mother had dragged her to when she was young, where women in various states of undress asked one another for marital advice and threw unwanted items onto a pile. She yanked her pants up like it was their fault they were so tight. In the mirror she gathered up her hair. One strand did not follow. She tried to brush it again and it fell back. Inching closer to the mirror, she saw the strand was connected to the front of her neck. A long hair was sprouting out of the middle of her neck. It was a monstrous length. She dug through her toiletry kit and found the tweezers. She plucked the hair and didn't notice where it fell.

The nine clicked to zero and Dorothy opened the app on her phone and waited to receive the call. When the therapist had first suggested a virtual session, Dorothy had assumed they would use FaceTime or have a "hangout," but the therapist had instead asked her to download a HIPAA-compliant messenger service called VSee. The fact that it rhymed with "VC" felt portentous but was probably coincidental.

The phone rang, or rather, the computer inside the phone manufactured a ringing noise. Life was increasingly filled with melancholy sounds like this, digital reproductions or replacements of analog sounds, reminders of historical periods gone by. One day these digital tones would not harken back to anything else; they would not be heard in reference to the past. But for Dorothy they were incomplete, shadow tones. Dorothy was of the generation that experienced the digital as a postscript to the analog and adulthood as a simulacra of childhood—a callback, flatly rendered, compressed into a narrower range of frequency.

The screen coughed up the therapist's chin and most of her neck. She was nodding and looking vacantly up, which meant, Dorothy knew, that she was looking at herself in the inset screen rather than "at" Dorothy—though what it meant to look "at" someone through the video format was no simple matter. In general, etiquette dictated that you keep your eyes relaxed and forward-gazing, with a pleasant half-smile on the lips. The therapist suddenly dropped down into focus, her face larger than it had been. She was probably doing this on her computer and had pulled the screen in closer, or moved her chair. Dorothy flipped her phone to the side so her own video was in the corner and the therapist was now stretched bigger. Her hair looked wet, like she had just gotten out of the shower or applied hair product, which made Dorothy uncomfortable, like a boundary had been crossed. The lines of her makeup appeared a little cracked, and when she opened her mouth, which she did before she spoke, out of fear of interrupting, because it was harder to gauge the length of silences over the distance, she looked unsure and stupid, something she had never appeared to be in person.

"Hi," the therapist said. "Can you hear me?"

Her skin looked different on the screen—thinner, dryer. Dorothy's eyes scouted the hotel room. There was nothing to look at. There should have been a painting somewhere, a child in a cornfield, a woman yanking her head off, but instead there was just a soft wall, slightly distended, stitched with black thread in a pattern reminiscent of a Tetris game, staring dumbly at her. She knew that some people only did therapy this way, but this was her first time. Her lips felt dry and like they might crack and bleed. She thought how appropriate it would be to begin bleeding from the mouth in virtual therapy. She stretched her mouth a little to see if she could get the bleeding started. Nothing. With her fingers up near her face she noticed the lines of dirt lodged under the fingernails.

"Hold on," said Dorothy, and moved from the chair, where she had been positioned at the table, to the bed, where she settled upright against a bank of pillows. The lighting here was worse but she couldn't move again without looking foolish. She found herself missing the African masks, the South American flutes. The video session was more mediated but also more restrictive. One was less free to look away. She trained her eyes on the black pinprick of the camera opening while she explained that she knew she was supposed to have something to say about being in Las Vegas but had nothing to say about being in Las Vegas.

"Why are you supposed to?" asked the therapist.

"I know I'm supposed to have, like, a 'take,'" Dorothy said, making and immediately regretting making air quotations with the fingers of her free hand.

Dorothy tried to make eye contact with her therapist, but

when she looked into the place where the eyes were, it was impossible, there was something wrong with it, the gaze wasn't returned. And anyway, her therapist's eyes were moving around all the time, darting around her office, thousands of miles away. Maybe they always did.

"There's a lot of . . . spectacle," Dorothy tried.

Her therapist's face froze mid-nod, with her mouth open. Her voice continued. "Do you enjoy the spectacle?" the voice asked.

"I'm losing you," Dorothy said, and then the therapist stuttered back to life.

"It's back," Dorothy said at the same time that the therapist said, "We can move to the phone," and then, "Oh, okay."

"There are interesting challenges to using this technology," her therapist said, peering into the screen with an intentness that she never displayed in their in-person sessions, as if the distance made it so they had to compensate with moments of more intimacy, greater scrutiny. Dorothy gave up trying to create the illusion of eye contact and talked to herself, addressing her professional anxiety to the square mirror in the corner of the screen. At last, there was a person listening who really got it.

The light in the room was changing as the sun traveled across the sky, burning holes in the clouds, and illuminating the room through the thin barrier of scrim, making her unattractively backlit. When Dorothy got up to close the curtains, she carried the phone with her.

"The last time we talked you had some concerns about your paper," the therapist said.

"Yeah," said Dorothy.

Her therapist looked at her blankly for what felt like a long time and then a wave of comprehension passed over her face as Dorothy's word, which must have been delayed, came through.

"How did it go?" she asked.

As a matter of fact, her paper had been very well received. But it was impossible to admit this, because the attention had been awful and so undeserved—all those people thinking that she had something to say when she knew that the ideas didn't hold together. The Christminster cookies, for example. Her paper went on and on about *ingesting* the city of Christminster, and when Dorothy delivered the paper, she did it like that, with an emphasis on the word "in-ges-tion," as if pronouncing the word slowly and emphasizing its syllables was the equivalent of having something to say about it. Dorothy's paper was filled, too, with rhetorical questions: *What is the meaning of this* ingestion? was how one long section began, a section that did not ultimately resolve the meaning of anything but indicated, by certain very long digressions about the Eucharist, baking, nineteenth-century discourses of the digestive tract, and the cholera epidemic, that the meaning, forever deferred and desirable, was profound.

Her therapist was waiting. She kept her head still, as if she didn't want to create unnecessary interference for the connection, but her eyes darted back and forth.

Dorothy shrugged. "Fine," she said. She remarked blandly that conferences were difficult, that she felt lonely without a respectable institutional affiliation, that she liked the Las Vegas architecture and the charming signage, that the presence of so much energy-inefficient neon light haunted her and made her feel closer to species death, and that being in constant air-conditioning made her bones ache. Then they talked about Dorothy's mother.

"It looks like we're—" her therapist said a while later, freezing. This time the picture did not stutter back to life. It was eerie seeing her caught like this, like catching her in dishabille; she seemed, not vulnerable, but less capable—a victim of time rather than a master of it.

Are you there? Dorothy would have said to the image on the screen, except there was a chance that the audio connection was still working, and she didn't want to sound desperate.

"I'm going to hang up now," Dorothy said instead, touching the red circle to end the call. As soon as she did another call came through, and she touched the green circle, which she couldn't stop thinking of as "picking up." They spoke only as long as it took to confirm that they had used all the time they had.

Playing for pennies in slotland was depressing, so Dorothy put fifty dollars on a plastic logo card. Fifty dollars was an amount she understood to be flushing away, and yet not an amount that would irreparably harm her or leave her feeling ashamed of profligacy, an amount equivalent to the amount she might flush away on any given night of eating or drinking. She chose a machine in unoccupied territory that accepted dollar credits, and whose design was a replica of an old-fashioned three-reel slot machine, where the numbers rolled around. But it was digital, as everything was. You touched a button on the screen instead of pulling a crank, and the game progressed very quickly.

It was noisy on the floor, even though there were no other players in Dorothy's immediate vicinity. The machines themselves, whether or not they were occupied, looped through various sound effects designed to entice passersby, rather the way that a crying baby gets himself fed. But the noise was background noise, soothing in its way, and receded as she settled into her play, as if Dorothy and her machine were enveloped in a private pocket of air. She had no interest in the other machines, was not moved to investigate their siren beeps and whistles. She was loyal to her machine; she had picked it out of all the others, and would not be tricked into jumping from slot to slot; that's how they got you, with the false hope that some other gamble might be more profitable than the one you had already lost on. Also, the other machines looked complicated; they involved multiple lines of betting; they were for experienced players. Dorothy knew her limits. She had been playing only a few minutes but had already pushed the button—she did the subtraction—thirty-five times.

There was no sensation involved at all, except when the touchscreen did not respond, causing her to jab her finger harder against the unresponsive—was it plastic? Some sort of microbead? Why did she think all the inorganic materials she couldn't name were made of microbeads?—careful not to jab too quickly, because the machine's sensitivity was such that it might lag or suddenly catch up to repeated touches, registering the loss of several dollars instead of one. On her next push, the lights flashed and the recorded noise of clattering coins cut through the ambient racket, alerting Dorothy that she had won five dollars. Intellectually she recognized that this win really represented a greater loss, but she could not deny the explosion of good feeling she felt up at the top of her skull, which she figured was the experience of feeling lucky.

"What are you *doing*?" said a woman in a voice so low that you would have mistaken her for a man if not for her strange laugh, which came out high and cackly, like a bird's chitter. The laugh had something automatic about it, suggesting that it was not controlled by conscious choice but was emitted due to biological or, perhaps, environmental factors, the sonic equivalent of a mating or migratory dance.

Dorothy pushed away from the machine and blinked, resisting the urge to rub her eyes. She did not want to give the impression of being woken from a haze. Her mouth felt dry. Weren't the people who worked here supposed to come around with free drinks? Or did that only happen if you were a high roller? She looked up and made a weak joke about Lydgate's gambling mania, and the woman, Judith Robinson, her former dissertation adviser, laughed again with the birdish cackle.

"Nice save, Dodo," she said, placing her hands on her waist in an exaggerated pantomime of discipline.

Judith was tall and gangly and bent over at an angle, like an ostrich ready to run. Her cheeks were lightly flushed and her lips were thick with fuchsia and her eyes had the shine of afternoon drinks. Dorothy knew Judith well enough to know she was not a drunk, merely an academic on holiday. It was typical, thought Dorothy—eyes taking in the unfathomable and helplessly rapt senior citizens feeding the slot machines with arthritic fingers, feet fighting the instinct to flee in panic as if from a fire—that her conversation with her therapist had happened just before running into the person who was more or less the reason she had gotten into therapy in the first place. The time, as ever, was out of joint.

"Let's get you out of this midnight sun!" Judith chirped, and clapped her hands like castanets above her head, an action that caused the sleeves of her kimono to billow dramatically. She didn't look back to check that Dorothy was following her. (Judith always operated in total confidence that her orders would be obeyed.) Dorothy fumbled to extract her card but pressed the wrong button or too many buttons and had no choice but to leave the card behind. The fifty dollars was, as she had predicted it would be, a waste, a wash.

To get to the Palazzo, where Judith was staying, they cut through the Venetian. Dorothy hadn't been inside any casinos other than Harrah's. She was shocked at the niceness of the Venetian. The Venetian was spacious and creamy. It was a beautiful mall with celestial ceilings. It was tacky, yes, but compared to the smoky low-ceilinged dark of Harrah's, this tackiness was effervescent; it made her feel weightless. Dorothy saw how attractive, in the right environment, blown glass could be.

It needed space. It couldn't be crowded. It had to be free to explode, fungally.

There were families everywhere, and everyone, even the children, carried shopping bags. And the drinks—the frozen, neon-colored, twisty-strawed drinks. There were waterfalls and tiles and from the bottom of every fountain, coins flashed. A huge sign spelled Love in glittery red letters.

"We forgot to hug!" said Judith, or actually, she sang it, like a doorbell chiming, making two syllables out of one. "Huh-ugh." She pulled Dorothy in. Dorothy's face collided with Judith's collarbone, a not unwelcome respite from Judith's aggressive eye contact, which she maintained even while walking in tandem, as if her eyes did not divide into the usual forward/peripheral functions, but had fully spherical, panopti-con-like mobility.

Dorothy liked hugging. Hugging was a way of demonstrating affection that also involved hiding your face. It had always been hard for Dorothy to look at Judith's face. There was something wrong with it. It was like a face that had buckled under too many surgeries, except that wasn't it at all; the face had its natural sags and its natural wrinkles. If some women's vanity compelled them to seek enhancement from the knife, it was the nature of Judith's vanity to preclude intervention. Surgery gave a face a spooky, cadaverous quality, whereas the problem with Judith's face was that it had too much life. It was like a living organism that sucked the life out of your face in order to sustain itself, so insatiable was its need for face-energy, which it took in through the greedy straws of Judith's probing, unusually round eyes. Her body had no smell. Dorothy knew from experience running her errands that Judith used a perfume that was so fancy that it did not layer artificial scent on top of human scent but somehow, through a patented combination of botanicals, neutralized the scent of the body entirely. (It ate it.)

"Stand there, I'll take your picture," said Judith, holding out a hand for Dorothy's phone, pushing Dorothy near the "canal," where employees in red scarves and striped shirts guided gondolas laden with shouting tourists. Everyone in the casino was shouting; it was the only way to be heard. "Now you can tell everyone you've been to Venice," Judith shouted, and Dorothy wondered how Judith knew that Dorothy hadn't been to Venice. Was it that obvious? Dorothy asked why Judith wasn't staying at Harrah's with the rest of the conference and Judith, instead of laughing, glowered a little and impatiently adjusted her kimono. Dorothy had always been guilty of making uninteresting small talk. That was probably why she had failed as a thinker: too much chitchat, too many conversations about the weather, the traffic, where were you born, what did your mother do?

Judith handed back the phone. It was a good photo. The lighting or something was flattering. Dorothy was grateful to have it. In every photo Rog took of her, there was something wrong with her face. It sometimes made her wonder if Rog didn't love her the way he said he did, if the bad photos he took were his way of expressing animosity. But that same logic would dictate that Judith loved Dorothy, and that couldn't be true.

"I love *Vegas*," Judith said, as if she could read Dorothy's mind. She waved a hand over her domain. "When the real Venice is underwater, this will be all we'll have. It won't be a question of *remembering* it or not. This will be Venice. This *is* Venice!"

For a moment Dorothy thought Judith was going to make them get into a gondola, but Judith turned, setting the parrots on the back of her kimono into flight, and announced her desire to sit by the pool at the Palazzo.

"Let's go home," Judith said.

"I want to hear all about you," Judith said. "Impress me."

There were eleven pools at the Palazzo. The one that Judith chose for their tête-à-tête was not long enough to swim laps and in a shape that Dorothy didn't know the word for; it was curved on two sides and straight on the other two, like a bone. They sat on plastic chaises and ordered piña coladas from a short, television-handsome waiter. The palm trees were sprightly and stiff, and had an incognito air, as if wearing wigs of fronds.

The temperature had plummeted since yesterday's spike. Dorothy and Judith kept their arms covered in cardigan/kimono. It was like they had stepped into a picture, like they were moving around inside the idea of a tropical paradise without actually risking any of the sunburn/discomfort of being in a tropical paradise. It was an experience of pure tourism, of the idea of tourism. Dorothy didn't really want to visit the tropics, anyway; she had political objections, and also, she did not like sand.

"Palm trees make me sad," said Judith.

Dorothy agreed. It was pleasant to agree with Judith, to be reclining on the plastic chaise, which was not a flimsy plastic, but a sturdy and luxurious plastic, a plastic that would be handed down from generation to generation. She was grateful they were not in a gondola. The waiter came by with their drinks, topped with huge chunks of pineapple. At last, a twisty straw of her own! She took a bite of fruit and the juice ran down her chin and she wiped it with a cocktail napkin. She said something idle about sustainability, how palm trees sucked resources from the desert environment, how, yes, that was a cause for sadness.

"That's not it," said Judith. Judith always had the ability to make Dorothy feel like a puppy who had crapped on the carpet. She wagged a finger like Dorothy was being mischievous or trying to get attention, but Dorothy was only ever trying to give the right answer. "It's that they're so far from home."

Back in graduate school, at the height of Judith's torture of Dorothy, when Dorothy routinely wept into Rog's arms at night over some slight or out of fear of Judith's rejection and omnipotence, Rog had happened to catch sight of Judith out in the wild. It had happened quite by chance. He and Dorothy were walking down Sixth Avenue on their way to a movie when they saw Judith heading toward them. As she walked, she was eating a piece of pizza, folded up in a paper plate, over a paper bag. Dorothy immediately pulled Rog off the sidewalk and into a CVS.

"That's the woman you live in fear of?" Rog had asked. "That woman who is eating pizza from a bag?"

If Dorothy squinted, she could almost see Judith as Rog did. Judith no longer held absolute power over Dorothy. They were two adults, not quite colleagues, but professional relations, reclining poolside, of their own free will, at a work function. Alas, equally true was that so long as Dorothy wanted Judith to send out letters of recommendation on her behalf, Judith was like a god or the weather or a weather god, a condition fixed and capricious that Dorothy had to endure and perform mysterious rites to placate. She could always rebel, of course. She could burn the bridge, treat Judith as the ridiculous self-important footnote that Rog believed she was—but that was easy for Rog to say; he hadn't read Judith's books. Judith's books were the reason Dorothy had gone to graduate school. Rebellion against Judith would be rebellion against Dorothy's whole life.

"I see what you mean," Dorothy said. "The palm trees *are* far from home."

Wavy teal lines painted on the bottom of the pool gave the water the illusion of dancing. A cluster of ambitious or optimistic women or perhaps just women who did not update the weather app daily shivered in bikinis and tiaras. Their discomfort was the homage or honor they paid to the bride among them, a jubilant pixie in a white sash that read SLUT. The SLUT dipped a toe into the water and declared it warm enough. At a command from her tanned lieutenant, festively attired in two strips of American flag, all the troops waded down the steps. They grimaced, shrieked, laughed, held hands. They looked like an advertisement for friends.

"I'm glad to see you," Judith said, in a voice that was newly thick. "I know that you'll understand."

In years past, whenever Judith had come to Dorothy with some problem that only Dorothy could understand, by which Judith meant, only Dorothy could solve, Dorothy had readily and eagerly thrown herself into the challenge. Usually the problem involved a computer file that needed to be retrieved from the downloads folder, or a scheduling conflict that had to be sorted out, or a course packet that needed photocopying. Occasionally it was something that Dorothy had to solve through an emotional maneuver; perhaps Judith needed her to agree that a rival in the department was being outrageous. Perhaps Dorothy had to type while Judith dictated a difficult letter sinking a junior professor's manuscript. More seldom it was an intellectual problem that needed sorting, such as recommendations on syllabus design; once, Judith had needed Dorothy to flesh out something she had said in seminar that later appeared, uncredited, in an article by Judith. This last transgression had occurred only once, and yet it seemed the most typical of Judith's excesses, insofar as it combined flattery, manipulation, outright domination, and coercion; no one could say Dorothy hadn't been a willing participant. Dorothy's friends had been outraged on her behalf, especially Micah, but Dorothy wasn't sure that the idea was, properly speaking, "hers": It had arisen in Judith's classroom, prompted by something Judith herself had said, about an article Judith herself had written; the idea, as Dorothy saw it, belonged to both of them, or rather, to neither of them, and all Judith had done was put her name on it first. Was being first a crime?

When Micah frowned, the corners of his mouth sank all the way to his chin, like a disappointed muppet. "You'll never get a job with that attitude," he had prophesied, perched atop a stone planter.

The luster of solving Judith's problems had somewhat faded since Dorothy had finished the program and discovered that having been Judith's not-favorite student didn't open any doors. Either Judith's name was worth less than it used to be, or Judith wasn't trying very hard to help her; Dorothy could never be sure. Still, the desire to please Judith, to earn her praise, was as strong as ever. Besides, Dorothy liked that Judith thought she would understand. So often Dorothy felt entirely alone; even with the people she loved most she felt encased in a diving bell or a clear plastic box, a cheap one, not like the sturdy plastic chaise she sat on now, and the things other people went around talking about and doing seemed objectively important and respectable but had no direct relevance to the circumstances of inhabiting her specific, disposable biodome. She was aware that putting it that way was an admission of gross privilege and elitism but such self-laceration only made the feeling of the biodome more pronounced. Dorothy had never really understood Judith, of this she was sure, but she appreciated being treated as if she did. It made her feel special, even as she knew that feeling special was the most perverse form the exploitation could take.

Today Judith was dealing with the problem of grief. Her longtime editor at Harvard University Press who had published all her seminal texts and others not so seminal had died in a freak accident. He had gone out for a walk on the Cape (his second home) at the height of the afternoon, when the glare off the water was most intense. His foot had lost contact with the rocky footpath, sending his body over the edge. He was discovered the next day by a group of high school students who had gone to a cove to smoke angel dust, a fact that had come out when the parents took a closer look at why their children were on the shore in the middle of the day instead of in school.

"Some people have been saying he did it on purpose, but that's because they can't accept the real tragedy: the accidental nature of the world," Judith said, motioning to the waiter for another round of piña coladas. "It's all very sordid."

Objectively that had to be so, although it was hard, while reclining in her luxuriously sturdy plastic chaise, poolside with a second piña colada on the way, for Dorothy to feel the impact of the story, to be there on the New England coastline with the angel-dust-smoking teenagers, the bloated editorial body, the cold gray ocean, the tragic inexorability of mischance. It wasn't that the pool seemed real and the dead body seemed false; it was that nothing seemed real.

"My friend died," Judith said, her voice rising in volume, a hammer taken to the surroundings. Dorothy waited for the picture to crack open and reveal them to be back in Judith's office, where the chair Dorothy had to sit in was a little lower than Judith's chair, and positioned to look at a portrait of Judith herself, which had been painted by a former student who became an art star in the 1990s, and which hung presidentially over her desk.

The picture world reverberated but held together. They were not on campus.

They were at the Palazzo.

One day this would be Venice.

"It's okay," said Dorothy, hoping that by lowering her own voice, Judith would feel inspired to also speak softly.

"No," said Judith louder and more insistently. "It feels good to cry. To let it all out."

With no regard for the tears welling in her eyes, Judith

accepted the drink the waiter offered and gave him her room number.

"It's on me," she said.

Such generosity was uncharacteristic. Judith must have been distracted by her tears, which were increasing. The physiological collapse, the lachrymal overflow, that, in a weaker person, would appear as weakness, in Judith only enhanced her strength. The watery sheen cascading down her face did not make her seem quavering or helpless but strong and passionate. She had the strength to cry; she had the force to withstand it. Tears were no match for her spirit. As the weeping increased in speed and volume, Dorothy braced herself for its sudden halt. It was not prudent to expect Judith to go on doing a thing or feeling a feeling simply because she was doing or feeling it with intensity. Judith, Dorothy knew, was one of those unusual people whose charisma and power to terrify are rooted in their unpredictability. Her majesty had a multiplying effect. Whereas some people govern by force of personality, she ruled by a kaleidoscope of personalities. And yet knowing this did not make Dorothy any more prepared to respond. Because even if Judith might do anything or be anyone, Dorothy was still just Dorothy.

The tears continued, punctuated by little hiccups and wheezing breaths. Dorothy marveled at the ease with which they flowed, as if they had been ready at the barricades, awaiting Judith's order. Dorothy reached out a pacifying hand but quickly retracted it, unsure of where it should go: On Judith's leg? On her arm? How high up on the arm? All the way to the shoulder? She patted the smooth plastic of Judith's chaise instead, and suggested that perhaps they could get Judith's mind off her personal tragedy by talking about work. Who was on Judith's panel? Judith snapped back that Dorothy was using a veneer of professionalism to mask her essential and regrettable callousness.

"What is the point of any of this," Judith asked, "if we can't be honest with each other?"

Judith imagined honesty as a kind of conversation: People were, or could be, honest with one another. She would relish a meta-conversation in which she could exert power while denying it. But honest conversation was pointless, because a declaration of feeling (*I hate you/I love you*) could never account for the myriad complications of Dorothy's relation to Judith, complications that manifested as emotional, even spiritual conflict, but were rooted in something material and intractable—their positions in the game. Judith was a teacher and a foster mother and an employer, and more than that, she was a node in a large and impersonal system that had anointed her a winner and Dorothy a loser, and due to institutional and systemic factors that were bigger than either of them—not more complicated, no, because no system is more complicated than a single human being—no one of Dorothy's generation would ever accrue the kind of power Judith had, and this was a good thing even as it was an unjust and shitty thing. Judith was old and Dorothy was young, Judith had benefits and Dorothy had debts. The idols had been false but they had served a function, and now they were all smashed and no one knew what they were working for. The problem wasn't the fall of the old system, it was that the new system had not arisen. Dorothy was like a janitor in the temple who continued to sweep because she had nowhere else to be but who had lost her belief in the essential sanctity of the enterprise.

"Your friend sounds like he was very special," Dorothy said.

"He had passion," Judith said, rooting in the pockets of her kimono for a tissue. Her tears had not stopped falling. "Which is more than I can say of most people."

Dorothy nodded.

"Now you try," Judith said, and blew her nose primly.

Dorothy sucked on her straw and was mortified to hear the slurping noise that indicated an empty drink. "What?" she said stupidly. The window of her brain was fogged with piña colada.

"Cry with me," said Judith. Her eyes were pink and swollen and glinting like the coins at the bottom of the Venetian fountains. Her lipstick had faded and her lips looked dry and naked. Of course Judith was aware that her lipstick had faded. But she wasn't going to reapply it. It was an act of will to refuse to reapply lipstick in front of another person. That kind of will was another form of domination.

Dorothy looked around at her fellow denizens of the poolside. No one from the conference was here. The other conference-goers were sitting in the ballrooms at Harrah's, or scrambling to finish their papers, or resting; maybe a few of them were on the Strip drinking or gambling, but they were not at the Palazzo, or not anywhere she could see. The women of the bachelorette party were still in the bone-shaped pool; they had the appearance of statues in a garden. Although they were smiling, their eyes looked far away and deadened with alcohol, and their mouths were twisted by effortful good cheer. It was so quiet that Dorothy could hear Judith doing something inside her mouth with her tongue, a bizarre little click that punctuated a low, almost inaudible whine, and reminded Dorothy of the sound of a new slide coming into the projector.

"Tears are the language of the body," Dorothy said, by which she meant that they could not be faked, but all Judith shouted was "I taught you that!"

Judith pointed around, gesturing widely, as if to draw to her all the space she could, to gather up everything she knew, which was everything, so she could dump it all over Dorothy, burying her with wisdom, experience, expertise. Looking up at the Palazzo tower, which was, Judith had told her on the walk over, the tallest building in Las Vegas, Dorothy tried to remember what had happened in her life that had led her to this point. She thought of Kafka's dog:

> *More and more often of late, thinking about my life, I seek out the decisive and fundamental mistake I have probably committed—and can't find it. And yet I must have committed it, because if I hadn't and had still not attained what I wanted to attain, in spite of the honest endeavors of a long life, then it would have been proof that what I wanted was impossible, and the consequence would be utter hopelessness. Behold thy life's work!*

Dorothy took a breath and exhaled and buried her face in her hands and did her best to channel the whimpering mewls of an infant. She thought about war and illness and climate migration and the saddest newspaper article she had ever read, about a man who regularly visited his Alzheimer's-ridden wife and her nursing home boyfriend; she didn't recognize her husband, but he never stopped coming, never told her who he—who she—really was. Privately, Dorothy felt proud of her effort. She had done a few school plays in her youth. She did not believe she entirely lacked talent for performance.

She moved her face to her elbow, and tried to wipe some spit into the corner of her eyes so that whenever she had to look at Judith again—which she hoped would not be for a very long time—there would be some physical evidence of distress. Dorothy's real cry was a quiet hiccupy thing—she had been told by men it was disturbingly soundless, and had occasionally been accused of faking it—so she made sure to be audible. As she increased her volume to a wail, the back of her throat opened a little and the crying became less kittenish, more committed to its own sense of aching futility and existential abandonment. She was almost there.

Judith broke off crying and burst into laughter. It wasn't

nasty laughter, there was genuine pleasure in it—the freedom of flight.

"I knew I could count on you to make me feel better," she said. Dorothy raised her head and saw Judith drying her eyes on a white pool towel. She leaned back her head, as if wanting Dorothy to admire the sinews of her long and youthful neck. She yawned, showing silver-filled molars, and announced that she needed a nap. Quickly Dorothy wiped her eyes with her fingers, rubbing away the saliva, and smiled like she was in on the joke. *Behold thy life's work!*

Judith made smacking sounds of goodbye near both of Dorothy's cheeks, said it had been wonderful to see her.

"Such a gas," she added. "You always slay me."

She dropped her used tissues into Dorothy's empty cup, and as she was leaving she turned back to say that she had high hopes for Dorothy's chances on next year's job market.

"You're special, Dodo," Judith said, as her kimono flapped its goodbye. "I've always told you that!"

The women of the wedding party noisily emerged from the pool, laughing and blaming one another for the cold. As the bride adjusted her sash and put on the floppy half-sweater that was known as a shrug, Dorothy sought out the decisive and fundamental mistake. It was not one decision she could blame, but all of them. She inhaled the cold air and felt in her left lateral incisor a sharp, definite ache. The ache began at the gumline and radiated down through the face of the tooth. There was an absence behind the pain; it lacked the dense surface area of, say, a molar. She thought that the pain would fade quickly, without anything to retain it.

That was wrong. In fact, as Dorothy discovered, the whole flat incisor is nothing but a surface for pain, a disc to receive and transmit it, or, more precisely, a surface of pain—the pain being not in, nor on, the tooth, but tooth itself. It was a shard of pain rather than a sliver of sensate bone that hung from

Dorothy's pinkish, slightly inflamed gums. She breathed harder, sucking air over the tooth, and the pain increased. She bit her lip and blinked rapidly to keep the tears from falling. It was no use. They poured down and spilled over her chin.

There was no tissue box to come to her aid. Dorothy didn't bother to cover her face. There was something fortifying about crying in public, about letting the snot flow; what felt degrading in private, in public announced one's sensitivity and the great passions that ruled a life. She dug around in her bag, which was always stuffed with napkins from whatever coffee shop she had last frequented. The napkin she turned up was thick and long, like a dinner napkin. She blew her nose with force, and something about the force knocked the pain off of her tooth, or maybe it had to do with the temperature in her mouth increasing (cold air could make teeth ache; warm air was a comfort), or maybe it was a meaningless coincidence of sensation. Maybe what happened inside her body had no relationship to what was outside it. She cried again, animally, whimperingly.

She dried her face. She folded the towel Judith had knocked to the ground when she departed and placed it on the chaise longue. The waiter hung back, through some combination of tact and disgust. A breeze rustled through the transplanted palm leaves. They made a noise like shushing.

* * *

Elyse: Let's go somewhere else to check out the vibe
Elyse: Harrah's is so depressing!

Dorothy was in bed and knew enough to know she could not survive another adventure on the Strip. She thought that maybe if she tried she could get herself back downstairs.

Dorothy: No I want to go to the oyster bar
Dorothy: It's here at Harrah's
Dorothy: It will be funny?!

Dorothy did not believe this, but as she expected, Elyse accepted irony as a reason to do something that she perceived to be well beneath her.

The oyster bar had no walls or windows or, god forbid, doors. It opened directly onto the casino. The hostess showed Dorothy, who had arrived first, to a table in the front next to a fake bush, where anybody could see her, but Dorothy wanted more seclusion. There weren't any tables "in" the restaurant, however—due to the previously observed lack of doors and walls and windows, the restaurant had no "inside" to speak of. It was a permeable zone, a gustatory oasis that bled into the territory of gaming. Dorothy sat at one end of the bar and tried not to look at the lobster tank on the wall next to her. She drank a Bloody Mary. The drink was spicy and strong. It cut through the sweetness of the afternoon's piña coladas, which, despite a nap and vigorous toothbrushing, had remained adhered in her mouth, or maybe just her memory. She didn't know what to do so she took out her phone, and she didn't know what to do with her phone, so she texted Gaby.

"Heyyyy," she texted, counting on the extra *y*'s to imply that her text was fun, that she was fine, that they were great friends, and that she was witty and debonair rather than an exhausted resin-spewing sack overwhelmed by the cold onslaught of vodka penetrating her brain.

Dorothy: I'm in VEGAS BABY!!!
Dorothy: [Person with Head Exploding Emoji]
Dorothy: [Knife Emoji]
Dorothy: [Crying and Laughing Emoji]

Gaby: If you're saying you killed your paper I know u did.

A pause. Dorothy looked around the restaurant, back to the screen.

Gaby: . . .
Gaby: Have you listened to your therapist's podcast?
Gaby: I can't stop thinking about it
Gaby: I'm dying to hear it
Dorothy: I can't, I'm just pretending it doesn't exist
Gaby: Sounds healthy
Gaby: I still think she should have YOU on it
Gaby: I think you're verrrrry relatable!
Dorothy: but not sympathetic
Gaby: SHE'S not sympathetic
Gaby: JK I don't know her
Gaby: She's just threatened cause you're smart
Dorothy: I dont think thats it but thank u for yr support
Gaby: Also it's like she's the mistress so of course she has to neg you a little
Gaby: to keep you interested so you don't dump her and go back to your main squeeze wife-therapist
Dorothy: mayyyybe?
Gaby: I know about these things!
Dorothy: I know
Dorothy: [heart emoji]
Dorothy: ok gotta go [another heart emoji]

Gaby was a good friend, but Dorothy was glad that the therapist hadn't wanted her on the podcast. It was the kind of thing she definitely would have agreed to and then massively regretted. The more she thought about it, the worse an idea it was—no matter how masked the details, someone would be sure to figure out it was her. How could she talk about Rog, her

mother, her students, *her body,* knowing it would be broad-
cast? Besides, her second therapist was sure to use the podcast
to raise the issue of her first therapist, and while Dorothy did
not believe she was doing anything wrong, in fact believed that
her therapeutic entanglements were proof that on some level
she was doing something right, that despite professional and
personal stagnation she had not entirely given up on the possibility of meaningful change, but was only deferring it to some
future date—still, she didn't need everybody knowing her
business. She didn't need to become an object of criticism.
That would make it even more impossible than it already was
for her to find a job. There was an argument to be made that
people who bared themselves in public helped others, that by
sacrificing their privacy they became examples to light the way,
but she didn't feel exemplary. There had to be something
wrong with whoever would do that, would strew their most
intimate thoughts and experiences around the world like
unopened bills. That should be the subject of the podcast:
"What Does It Say About You That You Have Agreed To This
Recording?"

She leaned against the wall but it wasn't the wall there, it
was the tank. Cold damp touched her through her cardigan.
Before she could look away she saw them, the lobsters, rubber-
banded claws scuttling silently, antennae waving, thrashing in
their green-gray antechamber to execution.

Elyse arrived and slid onto the next barstool. She was wearing a sleeveless jumpsuit with a plunging neckline and heels and
seemed not at all bothered by or even aware of the sub-zero
microclimate of the bar.

Dorothy was now in kissable distance from Elyse. Too
close. Angling herself at a more comfortable distance required
jamming the stool up all the way against the tank. She wedged
the stool back and forward and tried to avoid touching her

back to the tank and gave up and sank against it and too late realized that Elyse was waiting for her to answer a question. The question had probably been "How are you?"

Dorothy looked in either direction, as if the moment were a street she had to get to the other side of, and said "you know" in a tone that she hoped indicated that she was incredibly busy and dealing with complex and weighty intellectual matters that while she did not presume were of interest to Elyse, were definitely engaging and fulfilling—that she was an adjunct, sure, but, you know, not hooked up to a ventilator in "adjunct hell."

"I'm so glad to see you here," Elyse said. "But I wish we had been on the same panel. That panel in Texas was seriously the *best* one of my *life*."

Dorothy wanted to say something real about her admiration for Elyse, about clouds and botany and why people read and what teaching is for, but it was too early in their encounter to plunge in so deeply, so all she said was "Me, too!" Elyse asked about her paper, and Dorothy tried to keep the pep in her voice as she explained about the Christminster cookies.

"You seem anxious," Elyse said.

This sounded rude, but maybe it was merely forthright? "I was reading the news earlier," Dorothy said, which was true—rather than attend any afternoon panels Dorothy had spent the hours since leaving the Palazzo reading her phone and sleeping off the piña coladas—but she also hoped, by this reference to the unceasing rampage of current events, to explain any idiosyncratic or personal anxiety as the product of sincere sorrow at the looming extinction of the human race and to introduce a conversational thread that would lead them away from the morass of academic competition and toward something safe and neutral: the plight of humanity.

Elyse groaned. "Not you, too," she said. "I've had this conversation twice already today."

Dorothy ordered the surf and turf and sipped her Bloody

Mary but Elyse did not order a drink with her oysters. Dorothy wondered if she was pregnant or sober—at an academic conference, only pregnancy or recovery could explain someone not drinking—and was surprised to note how jealous and angry the thought of pregnant Elyse made her. It wasn't that she wished herself pregnant—more and more she believed the miscarriage to be some kind of divine intervention that had spared her the thing she most feared in life, making a choice—but she felt there should be something in life that Elyse didn't get. True, Elyse was divorced, and that was hard, but divorce was also a kind of glory. It announced that you had loved and been consumed in the flames, that you had lived; it made you serious and deep. That these were the thoughts of someone who had never been married or divorced was not lost on Dorothy, but what could she do? They were the thoughts she had. There was no other history from which she could speak.

While they ate, Dorothy interviewed Elyse about her new book and tolerated Elyse's questions about her paper. They had both finished their food when Elyse flagged down the bartender to ask for a glass of white wine. *Not pregnant,* Dorothy automatically tallied, hating herself for surveilling another woman, unable to stop herself from drawing a conclusion.

"Do you want another?" the bartender asked, and Dorothy, conscious of her excesses earlier that day, waved him away.

Elyse looked sternly at the saltshakers and announced that she needed Dorothy's help with a problem she was having with her neighbor. In the faintly perceptible affective shift, Dorothy realized that all conversation until now had been preamble; some main event was unexpectedly underway.

"I know we aren't really good friends," Elyse said, "but I respect you, and anyway it's good that we don't really know each other. I need the opinion of a neutral party."

"We know each other," Dorothy said, offended by Elyse's assessment. "I just told you about the Christminster cookies. I

only tell people I *really* like about those." She said it like it was
a joke but it was not a joke.

"You know what I mean," Elyse said, and laughed a little,
in a rapid, loud staccato. Dorothy had never seen Elyse nervous. She hadn't seen her most ways; they didn't really know
each other. She wasn't sure if Elyse needed her in particular, or
only needed someone, and she happened to be there, but in
either case, Elyse was here, and so was she. Gaby was right: It
was a good feeling, to be needed.

Elyse sighed. She seemed to be preparing herself. She
stared through the transparent Lucite half-wall that separated
the bar patrons from the kitchen. Flames leapt around the
edges of frying pans. After her divorce, she said—Dorothy had
heard?

"Yes," Dorothy said. "From Keith."

"Keith talks," said Elyse. She grinned. "He talks about you
sometimes."

"He does?" said Dorothy, pleased and trepidatious.

"Sometimes," Elyse said.

Anyway, Elyse said, after the divorce, she moved to a new
apartment. By great luck and a little effort, she had found an
apartment in a building inhabited by a friend who taught at
another university nearby. They weren't close friends at first,
but due to the geographic proximity and the professional connection, as well as Elyse's post-marital loneliness, the relationship quickly became close and intimate. Dorothy tried to con-
centrate on what Elyse was saying, but she was also wondering
what Keith had said about her. Did Elyse know about the night
in the cabin? Or did he just talk about feeling sorry for her,
that she was languishing while they were building bigger and
better tenure files, and if so, what did Elyse say in response?

"I wish there were more people like you there," Elyse said
suddenly, conceding defeat in her staring contest with the con-
demned lobsters behind Dorothy's head, and now looking

directly at Dorothy. "But most of my colleagues are career automatons; they can hardly talk about anything outside the profession. So this friendship with my neighbor is an important one to me. I don't make friends easily, especially not with women," she said, and here she gave Dorothy a look like that a deer gives to an automobile driver before being run over—a look of wounded vulnerability and fatalism that says giving up is preferable to failing to save oneself.

Elyse had been living in the building for a few months when her neighbor began having a lot of overnight visits from her boyfriend. Elyse got to know him, which was natural, since she and the neighbor spent so much time together, and the boyfriend was around, at first only a couple nights a week, but soon every night. At some point he moved in, although no formal announcement was ever made on this front; Elyse had the impression that his living situation was temporary or he was between places, and he and the neighbor seemed to treat it not as a formal cohabitation or stage in a relationship but in a more casual way; he was "staying there" was how it was explained to her.

"I should admit that I had a crush on him," Elyse said, "and that crush entailed the occasional sexual fantasy, but it was more that I liked being around him. He was funny and in addition to being funny, he clearly thought *I* was funny, and we had similar taste in music, which we bonded over, because his girlfriend, my friend, has more or less stopped listening to new music altogether. There was no reason for her to do that and in fact she complains about it a lot, the way she and music have parted ways, but she acts like it was inevitable, or a health condition, rather than a choice she was making and continuing to make."

Elyse took a last swallow of wine. Dorothy, who since turning thirty had also more or less stopped listening to music, which had come to feel like a psychic intrusion, an unwelcome alteration of natural equilibrium, nodded, and wished she had paced herself with the drinks better, because then she could be ordering another drink now.

As time went on, Elyse started getting more and more of a vibe from the boyfriend. Sometimes it felt like all three of them were living together in some kind of polyamorous or boundary-pushing *Three's Company*–type relationship, because again, though Elyse didn't live in the same apartment, she was often visiting, or they came over to her place, or they lingered in each other's doorways, talking, reluctant to separate. It wasn't that she was hoping to break up her friend's relationship, although, she said, it would have been a kindness if someone had, because the friend and the boyfriend fought constantly and about anything. They were one of those couples that can't pick a restaurant without devolving into a meta-argument and sometimes when Elyse came home she could even hear them through the door, which she passed to get to her apartment (she lived two floors above). She couldn't hear particular words or the content of a fight, but she could tell, from the high-pitched rolling female cadences and the occasional sound of a hand smacking a table for emphasis, that there was, as the saying goes, trouble in paradise.

There was one night in particular that Elyse thought her ethics might totally collapse. Her friend was visiting family in Ontario, and Elyse and the boyfriend had gone out with some other mutual friends to see a band, the kind of thing the friend was always refusing to do with him. It was after midnight and the others had piled into a cab, but Elyse and the boyfriend said they would take the bus—"to save money."

"It was as if by some implied contract we wanted to be alone together," said Elyse, "although of course we weren't alone, we were in a very public place. But I think that was part of it, too. We wanted to extend our time together but we didn't want to be isolated, in a situation where we might actually betray my friend."

It was a very long wait for the bus, which ran only once an hour at that time, and the longer they sat there, waiting on a dirty graffitied bench in the bus shelter, the more Elyse had the feeling that she and the friend's boyfriend were already a couple—not a couple of long standing, perhaps not even a monogamous couple, but she could see how they must look from the outside, like a couple who should have taken a cab but for politics or economics or pathology had committed themselves to public transportation and were waiting for the bus home, where they would fall asleep, entangled or not, together in the same bed. In the morning one of them would bring the other one water, or coffee, and they would look at the headlines. Like couples do.

"I don't usually think people want to kiss me," Elyse said. "I know I can come off as a snob, but I really don't have a very high opinion of myself. But I was sure that at any moment my friend's boyfriend was going to kiss me. I braced myself for it. I was ready. I swear his head moved toward mine. But then, all at once, after all that time, the bus arrived, and we got on it, and the moment passed. I felt it dissolving, time reorganizing on the other side of this kiss that never happened."

Shortly thereafter the friend discovered that the boyfriend had been cheating on her with his co-worker, and after many fights and tears and one doomed attempt at reconciliation, the relationship ended. Elyse was devastated that the boyfriend had been having an affair—on her friend's behalf, yes, but also, if she was honest, she was devastated that the affair wasn't with her. Now that she knew that the boyfriend was capable of that kind of deception, she felt like they had wasted a lot of time, and maybe their only chance. Then she found out that the affair with the co-worker had ended as soon as the relationship with her friend ended; it hadn't been love at all, merely a breakup strategy. But by now of course she could not violate the trust of her friend, who she sat with, night after night, consoling her, analyzing her heartbreak. She stayed "friends" with the boyfriend, now ex-boyfriend, but she kept her distance, probably because she did not trust herself.

"I never would have violated her trust," Elyse said again, and then, suddenly, "Oh hi, Edward." She jumped up and excused herself to greet an older man who had just come into the restaurant. Dorothy recognized him as a professor from Berkeley who would be delivering the keynote lecture, on a theory that emphasized "the episodic" as a virtue with radical political utility rather than a failure to achieve "continuity" or "coherence." He was accompanied by several distinguished-looking men, and one young woman who Dorothy knew to be his former graduate student and current fiancée. Dorothy looked at her phone. No texts. She checked her email. A bill from the gas company. She refreshed it again to make sure nothing new had come in in the time it had taken her to open and close the gas bill without reading it. There was nothing. She then refreshed a third time, not expecting anything, just because she didn't want to stare at the conversation she had not been invited to join and because her finger made the motion of its own volition, a step in a dance to music only the finger could hear, and then Elyse was back, adjusting the clasp of the thin gold chain she wore around her neck.

"Do you know Ed?" she asked, and when Dorothy shook her head, Elyse said that she would introduce her next time.

"Where was I?" she said, sounding as if she genuinely did not remember.

"You never would have violated your friend's trust . . ." Dorothy said, and Elyse agreed eagerly.

"No, of course not," she said. "Never."

Dorothy said that she would not have expected otherwise. At this reassurance Elyse looked a little disappointed, as if what she wanted was not to be found blameless but to be exonerated for having sinned in her heart.

Because Elyse was still "friends" with the ex, insofar as they had not declared themselves enemies or unfollowed each other on the digital platforms where so much contemporary life transpired, some months later he included her in an invitation to a party at the place where he was living his bachelor life, a huge loft where the roommates projected films and skateboarded through the rooms they had built out of plywood. It was the kind of place that Elyse's friends had lived in when they were in their twenties but had outgrown, and while it was fun to revisit, the atmosphere confirmed Elyse's belief that she and the ex, no matter the thickness of sexual tension between them, were on different life paths and could have been no more successful as a couple than her friend had been with him.

"I might as well tell you who the friend is," said Elyse, draining her glass. "It's so cumbersome to keep it shrouded. Her name is Alexandra. I think you both worked with Judith Robinson?" In addition to this drama that she was explaining, Elyse added, she had felt some professional tension with Alexandra, which they both suppressed admirably, concerning Elyse's success. Alexandra's book draft had received scathing readers' reports, and the first press she was with had dropped it, but she had finally found the right publisher, which made Elyse, she said, "so happy for her."

"I had no idea she had trouble with her book," said Dorothy, sitting up too quickly. She had been leaning on the bar with her head cradled in her hand and now something buzzed in her ears and darkness swam in splotches before her eyes and then the room went completely black; she blinked and her vision cleared. "That's terrible."

If this came out more anguished than she meant it to, it was because while Dorothy was pleased to learn of Alexandra's troubles, she was also dismayed, because if the system didn't work for Alexandra, then she, Dorothy, was even more fucked than she had believed. This wasn't to say that Dorothy believed that Alexandra was more deserving of a job than she was. It was just that Alexandra was more suited to a job than she was. She was cut out for it. She was what the world wanted. She was the way of the world.

"She'll be fine," said Elyse, misreading the combustion roiling under Dorothy's skin. "Her chair likes her."

Still, Elyse was always aware that jealousy and competition were buried deep in her relationship with Alexandra and probably always would be. The jealousy and competition had been compressed by time and pressure into a geological sublayer. Building on top of this layer was possible, but it was like building a swimming pool on a hillside; you needed a retaining wall.

"It goes without saying," Elyse said, "that you have to swear to put all this in the vault. The book stuff, too."

Dorothy put a hand on her heart and swore it.

At this point the bartender came over and Elyse requested another glass of wine for herself and one for Dorothy.

"I can't handle it that you're not drinking," Elyse asked. "It makes me feel so ill-mannered, just talking on and on."

"No, no," Dorothy said, but she didn't know who she was saying no to—Elyse, to assure her that it wasn't rude of her to talk on and on; the bartender, to say she didn't want the wine; or herself, to say that it was fine to go ahead and have the drink. If her no was directed to the bartender it was too late. He was already pouring the wine. She and Elyse waited, as if by tacit consent, for him to lift the glasses over the transparent Lucite half-wall, and when he went away again, Elyse picked up the story. The wine was terrible: cloying and heavy. Dorothy drank a big gulp, and then another. If this was something she had to get through she might as well make a dent in it now, so as to take it easy later. The second gulp was slightly less terrible.

Elyse explained that at the party she was feeling down in the dumps and ugly. It was around the time that she was finishing a big fellowship application, and she had been bingeing as a way of coping with the stress. Chocolate was her weakness. "What a cliché, I know." She wound up talking for a while with the ex-boyfriend's identical twin, who she knew slightly. The twin was an aspiring documentary filmmaker who worked for a branding agency, but the conversation wasn't especially interesting; they didn't have much in common despite their both being interested in culture and movies and things of that sort. Elyse had always found the twin to be better-looking than Alexandra's ex, but in a subtle way, because, of course, they're twins. Anyway, the twin had romantic drama of his own at the party, and at some point remarked morosely that *his* ex was leaving with another man.

"Here I did something I've never done before. It truly shocked me," said Elyse. "Which is that I looked right at him and said, 'You can go home with me.'"

The next thing she knew, she was in a cab, stopped in traffic, because it was a weekend night, which gave her and the twin plenty of time to silently and individually contemplate their decision while making idle chitchat about gridlock. They didn't touch each other at all in the car but as soon as they were in the apartment turned to each other with starving mouths and had sex three times in a row.

"Three times!" Elyse said. "I mean, *that's* something my ex-husband never did."

Dorothy nodded sympathetically, hoping her nod communicated not that she identified with this particular complaint, not that she was revealing anything about Rog and what he was or wasn't capable of, but simply that she was a woman and Elyse was a woman and she, Dorothy, was sympathetic to the plight of all sexually unsatisfied women, which they both, at various moments whose exact times were vague and whose exact causes unspecified, had been.

The thing Elyse most remembered about the sex was that he liked to finish standing up, and she didn't expect it to work, because he was shorter than her, but she sort of crouched into a standing squat and it was fine; by the third round, she joked, she was ready for the Olympic team.

The real drama came the next morning, when Elyse had to figure out how to get the twin out of the building without running into Alexandra. "How psychotic would she think me," Elyse said, sipping the wine with no indication that she found it unpleasant in her mouth, "to have slept with her ex's twin?" It would have appeared she hated Alexandra, or wanted to steal her life, when nothing could be further from the truth. "I like *my* life," Elyse declared. Elyse and the twin rose early, drank coffee, and ate frozen waffles. They had sex again. Elyse worried she would get a UTI, and in fact, she did.

"Ugh," said Dorothy. "I had one that lasted six weeks once."

"That's horrible," said Elyse.

"I did it to myself. I didn't go to the bathroom," said Dorothy.

"Sometimes you just don't want to get up," said Elyse.

Around nine, Alexandra's ex-boyfriend, who had seen them leave the party together, a fact not lost on Elyse at the time, texted his twin to ask if he was with Elyse, and the two of them leaned back against the pillows and laughed about it.

"I've never had a threesome," said Elyse dreamily. "But this text made it like a psychic threesome. It was obvious to the twin that I had slept with him as a way of sleeping with his brother, and obvious to me that he had slept with me as a way of bonding with his brother. And of course Alexandra's ex knew everything. I should have found this disgusting but I didn't, it felt almost familial, really sweet. Everyone had gotten something they wanted, even Alexandra's ex, who got the confirmation that I believe he was always looking for, of how I had found him desirable. And I got the confirmation I wanted, because he was clearly jealous. It was all very romantic."

They decided the twin would leave after twelve, so that if he ran into Alexandra on the way out, he could say that he came by to borrow a record or something; it would be fishy, but it would be late enough in the day that it could somehow be explained away. So during the whole morning they sat around talking, and drinking more coffee, and watching clips on the Internet, and listening to music, and in general enjoying the decadent fortune of a slightly extended one-night stand. Elyse started to fantasize that this could work out, that the twin could be her boyfriend, that maybe the whole reason the ex had come into her life was to bring her to the twin. Over the course of the morning the twin told her that his—their— mother was a triplet, which made sense, seeing as multiples run in families, and that his mother had been adopted, separated from her siblings at birth and recently reunited with them.

"I saw a documentary like this," said Dorothy, and Elyse nodded.

The twin wanted to make a short film about his family, had started shooting some interviews, just rough stuff, to test out the idea. He said he would show Elyse a clip of something he had shot on his phone, of his mother and her sisters—his aunts—talking about their favorite foods and vacation spots; it was, he said, uncanny how alike they were.

But while he was swiping back to find the clip, he swiped through a photo, and it was Alexandra, and she was topless.

"The thing I most remember is not her nipples," said Elyse. "I would have guessed it would have been the nipples, since I'm always curious about nipples; they're so different on everybody. But it was her face. She looked so free. She's probably my best friend—not like my *best* best friend, not better than childhood friends, but she's the person I spend the most time with day in and out—and I realized I had never seen her happy. It made me wonder if there's something about me that makes her unhappy, like if there's an observer problem, where if I'm looking, she's guaranteed to be morose, or at least ambivalent.

"It turned out that Alexandra had had a fling with the twin," Elyse went on, "sometime just after she and the boyfriend broke up. It wasn't serious, and the ex never found out, but that was the real reason he was afraid of running into her in the building—it wasn't about me at all.

"The problem," she said, and here Elyse looked down and realized that the jumpsuit had slipped too low, so she stood up a little to tug it back over her shoulders, "is that ever since I found out that she slept with the twin, I've been consumed with hatred for her. It's been a month and I keep making up excuses to not see her. I can tell that she's upset about it, and confused, and I know she deserves an explanation, but I just can't stand being around her; it makes me feel so guilty and ashamed. Not that I did anything wrong. I really don't think I did anything wrong. But I could tell, from the way she looked in that photo, that they had a connection that I didn't have with him. I thought the sex had been great, it had made me feel so good. But it was sort of . . . abstract. It was like it was happening to somebody else. Not in a bad or dissociated way, it just didn't feel like real life. After seeing that photo of Alexandra, I know that my face never looked like that. I feel like she took something away from me that I can't get back. And I miss my friend. I miss her so much."

With that Elyse reached for her wine and almost knocked it over but steadied it. She drank and grimaced, as if noticing the flavor for the first time. Dorothy wanted to tell Elyse that she deeply identified with her story, which she understood as a poignant, if slightly rambling, commentary on shame, on the interruption of a pleasure. Whether or not she knew it, Elyse's story was a parable about academia and what it did to pleasure, how it took the most simple and innocent desires—to tell stories, and stories about stories—and made them ugly. Dorothy, who for so long had felt flattened and oppressed by Alexandra's shamelessness, by her professional security and her easy assumption of achievement, was pleased to have a comrade in her shame, a person who was, like herself, a victim of Alexandra—not a witting one, of course; Alexandra did not actively wish harm to Dorothy or Elyse; Dorothy was not paranoid. But there was a way in which Alexandra's ease routinely put others into shadow, and in the case of Elyse's story, Alexandra's pleasure, which was so vital that not even a photograph could destroy it, had destroyed Elyse's. Dorothy had heard of people whose pleasure existed free of concern with other people, whose lives were not dictated by comparisons, jealousies, and rivalries, and they seemed to her narcissists and sociopaths, completely out of joint with the social, which took as its participatory condition spite as well as joy. And yet just knowing that Elyse—beautiful Elyse, who studied clouds and flowers, who dressed fashionably and whose career was more ascendant than Alexandra's own (Dorothy was still ingesting the news that Alexandra's professional march had not been as unimpeded as she had believed)—just knowing that Elyse, too, was subject to having her happiness wrenched away by someone else's greater, purer, and more coherent happiness, this somehow gave Dorothy comfort, like she was not alone in shouldering the burdens of life.

"I've been reading about shame with my students," Dorothy began. "You know that Tomkins defines it as the *interruption of a pleasure*—"

Here Dorothy noticed that Elyse was smiling goofily at her phone.

"Sorry," said Elyse, texting. "It's this guy I just started seeing." She looked up again. "You were saying about . . . pleasure?"

There were people who would have been angry at this obvious breach of etiquette, but Dorothy was mostly humiliated by her own pedantry. Why had she tried to turn this into a teachable moment? Elyse didn't need her "reading" of the situation. She just wanted someone who also knew Alexandra to listen to her and tell her she wasn't a bad person.

Dorothy patted Elyse's hand. "You're not a bad person," she said.

"I don't think I'm a bad person," said Elyse. "And I know that anyone I sleep with is going to have slept with other people. I just don't want to know *who* those other people are."

"What other people have doesn't take away from what you have," Dorothy said, saying what she knew was the right thing to say, the helpful thing, even if she didn't think it was true. "You had your own special thing with him."

"The truth is I want them both for myself," said Elyse. "And I don't have either."

Elyse opened her purse and said she had forgotten her wallet. She apologized too many times, making the situation worse by exaggerating the hardship she was inflicting; the pity she felt for Dorothy was palpable. Dorothy put down her credit card and went to the bathroom. Nothing. No blood on the paper. There was no evidence of the clot from earlier in the day. Maybe it had been a hysterical symptom. The idea of a hysterical symptom, she thought as she rinsed her hands in the sink, was the sort of thing that she could never bring up with Rog, who would accuse her of self-hatred, when all she was, was curious, and eager to assign some signification to what on another level she knew was brute and meaningless physiology.

She started talking as soon as she had a hand on the barstool.

"It's scary to think, *That could have been me*," she said. "That's what the story is about, isn't it? Contingency? You could be Alexandra, and she could be you?"

Elyse looked up from her phone with fearful eyes. Maybe it was the confusion of alcohol, but a person suffering a temporary amnesia might also look as Elyse did now, smiling vacantly to buy a few more seconds, opening her mouth and closing it without speaking. Dorothy thought about the ravages of age, dementia, Alzheimer's, introducing yourself every day to the person you know best in the world, who knows you not at all.

"It's Dorothy," Dorothy said, and watched as Elyse, like a sleepwalker shaken to consciousness, resettled into her usual expression of dreamy half-amusement.

"Oh god," she said, "I don't know what's wrong with my brain, but when I looked up at you I thought you were Alexandra, and that you had overheard our whole conversation. Which is crazy, 'cause I know Alexandra isn't at this conference. She's visiting her mother. Her mother has ovarian cancer."

"Jesus," said Dorothy.

"I know," Elyse said.

She added, "It was like there was a scrim between your face and my brain, or like I had clicked on the wrong file."

Dorothy said that that was exactly what Elyse's story had been about, someone who clicked on the wrong file and revealed an image that had changed everything. They parted with hugs and kisses.

"Good luck with job stuff in the fall" was the last thing Elyse said, "let me know how it goes," and with this reference to Dorothy's lowly status and the market's vicissitudes, whatever bonds had formed in their time together separated and curdled. Dorothy stayed up late in the hotel bed, ragefully clicking around her phone, reading the headlines, "liking" new pictures of her friends and their vacations, their kids, their pets, the signs and vanity license plates they photographed because they were funny, their cats in costumes, their dinners, their beautiful plants, glossy with green health.

At five o'clock in the morning Dorothy, idling in the lobby, opened the ride-hailing app and selected the shared-ride option, because, after spending fifty dollars on her slot card and treating Elyse to dinner, she had decided to live as deliberately as possible, at least for a day or two. She watched the icon of the car make its crawling digital approach and went outside to see it, life-size, roll along to the side entrance of Harrah's. She took the seat behind the passenger seat and slammed the door.

"Just getting one person after you," said the driver, who resembled a volcano, dark-jacketed and pyramidal, topped with a red fedora. They headed south on the Strip.

Dorothy looked out the window. *I am leaving Las Vegas,* she said to herself. That was a movie she had never seen. She thought of the book *Learning from Las Vegas;* she owned it, of course, but she had never read it. It was just another false start, another purchase toward the identity of a person she had turned out not to be. The sky was blue-dark but the streets were flooded with light from the casino signs. The late-night/early-bird walkers were wobbling in big groups; some looked confused, some wretched. Gigantic half-naked women flashed by on buses and taxi roofs, hurrying to get home. These advertisements, which had seemed so trashy and garish in the daytime, melted into the pre-dawn and left no trace. Dorothy felt peaceful, like she was being driven briskly and efficiently in a submarine through hell. She thought again of John, of his vision on the island of Patmos. So many afternoons as a child she had hidden under her bed, reading and reread-ing Revelation. It seemed impossible now that hell would be so grotesquely baroque. It must be barren.

She prepared herself for her final glimpses of the Eiffel Tower and the Statue of Liberty, hoping that whatever had been unsatisfying and dull about her encounter with the jumbled array of kitsch earlier in the trip would be resolved, that as they speeded away she would look behind her and come to a more complete understanding of what Las Vegas was and had been for her. Then she heard the clicking of the turn signal and the car glided onto the highway, leaving the Strip behind. She looked at her phone and realized they had been going north, not south.

Dorothy's sense of direction was not good. She and Rog used GPS whenever they rented a car; neither of them trusted her to navigate.

Then, as quickly as the car had gotten onto the highway it was off again. As it turned into a casino driveway, it began to dawn on Dorothy that a shared ride was literally shared—that someone else was going to get into the back seat next to her, a stranger who was not, like her, soberly on their way to the airport to get the cheapest available flight, but a stranger who had been out all night drinking or fondling strippers, activities which were not in themselves necessarily wrong but that would introduce a new element into the car ride, and more specifically into the area directly adjacent to herself—when a white boy in an orange polo shirt with a blurry round face who looked to be no more than fourteen bounced into the front passenger seat and slammed the door. The smell of beer emanated from him; if he had been a cartoon character, the artist would have drawn him with x'd out eyes and smell lines to indicate the stench.

"Sup," he said to the volcano, who responded with a languid "sir" in his direction, and asked how he was. Through chattering teeth the boy said he was "Amazing."

He was in "Vegas" for a long weekend with his fraternity, he said, from the University of Kansas. Dorothy always hated meeting anyone from Kansas. They always had to say something about her name. But the boy didn't turn around and introduce himself, and she didn't reach through the seats to extend a hand. The hair on the back of his head looked clean and soft. Dorothy wondered what had happened to his jacket. Or did the fraternity have some rule forbidding sleeves? Vegas was weird, he said. He spoke with the slow emphasis of someone who is afraid that if they aren't careful the slur of their words will get stuck together and never again come apart.

The car pulled away from the casino. Traffic was light at this hour. There was a park, and parking garages. Dorothy remembered that the airport was close; they couldn't be more than a few minutes away. Then they made a right and were back on the Strip. They passed a house-size pedestal and Dorothy craned her neck up as the Statue of Liberty vanished out of view. She was now thoroughly disoriented and had missed her opportunity to take in the replica statue as an aesthetic experience or form any coherent impression of it. It was behind her. To say her impression was in pieces would imply it was broken, when in fact, it had never been assembled.

"I have to tell you," the boy said out his window, his accent flat as the fields of his ancestral home, "I've seen some things."

There were boys like this in Dorothy's classes, and when she thought about what they did over the weekend, her imagination ran to predatory drunkenness thick and slow, but she pictured it contained in basements or dorm rooms, rather than out loose in the world. There was something about encountering this kind of collegiate drunkenness out loose in the world that made it feel less threatening and more pure of heart. The boy, she could tell, was exceedingly pure of heart. There was something tender and vulnerable about him and she longed to protect it. But that made him worse, more sordid and contemptible. This naïve boy had driven across the country with his teenage brethren on a mission to drink until puking—these were all assumptions, that they had driven, that they were underage, that someone had thrown up, if not him then one of his friends, and she felt justified in making them—in order to issue solemn proclamations on what was weird, on what had been seen. This was the problem with America. This boy's innocence, which was his privilege. And why was he alone? Had he been abandoned by his group? Whatever happened to brotherhood?

"We went to a club tonight," he said. "I'll tell you. It was a strip club. Nothing happened. My buddies are gentlemen. But there was this girl, or she said she was a girl, but I don't think she was a girl."

There was a titillated exuberance in his voice. He looked out the window.

"I don't think she was a girl," he said again, like his words had gotten stuck in a groove and would continue to play there until someone came along and nudged the needle to the next track.

Dorothy waited for the real confession to drop, for him to admit the theft, the assault, the gang rape. But the silence thinned out into nothing. There was no crime, no revelation. There was only wondering misperception.

"I guess you're not in Kansas," said the volcano, and the boy chuckled good-naturedly, and Dorothy pictured her hands wrapped murderously around both of their ignorant throats.

"Not in Kansas," the boy said.

"That's the truth," the boy said.

The boy loved his home state. A lot of people moved away, but he didn't want to. He had a pickup truck, he said.

"You probably don't know anyone with a pickup truck," he said.

The volcano remarked that, on the contrary, he knew several people who drove pickup trucks.

"You do?" said the boy, ecstatic. "Really?"

Past the Hard Rock Café they turned left, and continued on into the neighborhood around the university. The boy talked about a documentary he had seen about genetically modified crops. He mentioned that the government was keeping information from them, the American citizens. There was a paranoid implication there that reeked of Internet subcultures. There was a betrayed incredulity. The car pulled up at a beige apartment complex where a flag with Greek letters was hanging out the window.

"This is it," the boy said, although the gearshift was already in park. "See our flag?"

"Thanks for the ride," he said, with deep earnestness, as if it had been a great favor and kindness to pick him up, an effect enhanced by the lack of open commercial transaction, the fee being electronically paid by the credit card company, "thank you so much, you take care, sir," and Dorothy thought his mother, wherever she was, and however she felt about him being out at the strip club alone until sunrise, would be proud of his manners.

As he shut the door, he turned his face toward the back of the car, and saw, for the first time, Dorothy sitting there. Her presence passed into his understanding and as it did, the shadow of absolute terror passed over his face. It seemed to happen slowly but it must have taken mere seconds, because the car was already turning away. The look on the boy's face was something Dorothy had never seen on any human face. It was a little like the look of stricken misrecognition Elyse had given her last night at dinner but in another way it was nothing like it. Elyse had appeared to be bewildered, as if she knew what she was seeing could not be real; she had simply needed help sorting out what she knew on some cognitive level to be a sensory malfunction. The expression of this boy could not be corrected with information because the information would come from too far off the grid of recognizable fact. He had not seen the wrong person; he was seeing someone where there had been no one, a material presence, a ghost, and the ghost was her.

She lifted a hand and waved and was conscious of a grin working its way into the corners of her mouth. She was conscious that she was finally having fun. The boy's mouth fell open and his eyes widened and his eyebrows crawled fearfully under his hairline and he stood there, getting smaller, as the car turned back to the road on its way, without any further interruption, to the airport. The boy staggered a little. He did not wave back.

That was Las Vegas.

G aby was having a party in her apartment, which occupied the third floor of a townhouse by the river.
Technically, it wasn't "hers." She and Brian were the
discounted tenants of her all-seeing parents and the cash
investment they had made fifteen years ago. Brian was always
talking about moving—he wanted independence, he would
say—but he couldn't deny the advantages of staying put. The
baby's room was the first door on the left, separated from the
rest of the apartment by a long hallway, an ideal layout for
when Gaby and Brian wanted to sit in the living room talking
or watching television, but unideal for visitors, who had to tip-
toe, coat in hand, past the danger zone. But tonight the baby
was on the Upper East Side with Gaby's parents, and no one
had to worry about noise.

"HELLO," Gaby shouted every time she opened the door,
just because she could. Dorothy had expected Gaby to feel sad
or worried about the baby, but Gaby's eyes were shining with
joy, and wine. She had a new haircut and her dress was immod-
estly short and she reeked with determination to enjoy the
night. Rog went into the kitchen to deposit a bag of beer, and
Gaby, hopping from foot to foot as if her feet were on fire,
dragged Dorothy into the baby's room. It smelled sweet like
baby shit and something else, baby lotion. A mobile of air-
planes sentenced to an eternal patrol circled the ceiling above
the empty crib.

"Look at it!" Gaby said triumphantly. "Look! I. Am. Free!"

There was something haunting about a child's room with no child in it. It conjured sudden death, hushed voices, tragedy, shoes never worn. But Gaby was hyped up. She twirled a little and jumped up and down on the padded mat of animal faces. She pointed to an unblinking white camera positioned between a blackout curtain and a shelf where a monkey, a dog, a dinosaur, and an elephant crowded in a row, like a bizarre evolutionary experiment waiting to have its mug shot taken.

"It's off," Gaby said of the cyclops on the wall. "When it's on, I can't stop watching it. It's the greatest TV ever. He barks like a seal. But now I get to talk to *you*. An *actual adult*."

A child's world was comprised of machines with faces and well-intentioned wild animals. Why were stuffed animals cute and human dolls creepy? Dorothy looked around for the hippopotamus she had bought as a baby gift and didn't see it. Maybe it was so special that it had gone with Sherman on his grandparents' sleepover, or maybe Gaby had forgotten who it was from and given it away, or maybe she had remembered and given it away anyway.

When they were younger, Gaby had smoked cigarettes to have something to do with her hands. She had been an awkward and unattractive smoker, always holding the cigarette too close to her face between short, enthusiastic puffs, which she seemed to take into her lungs not by inhalation but by the reverse; it was a jabbing motion, like smoking was her way of punishing the cigarette for existing. *You asked for this* was what it looked like. Dorothy was glad when Gaby gave it up, though Gaby had not outgrown the need to always be holding or fondling some security object. That habit had become less obvious since everyone had acquired it vis-à-vis their phones, but Dorothy still noticed it, perhaps because it was accompanied by the music of the dozen bangles that pharaohnically lined Gaby's arms: the enthusiastic tinkle of picking up and putting down coasters or hair elastics or shredding napkins, and then, the clunk when she caught herself, briefly folded her hands, girl-like, in her lap. But the hands always broke free again. Currently they were picking up and putting down Sherman's sheep rattle, getting it into a row with three other rattles, all of which featured heads of different animals on cloth sticks. She was a warlord. She had decapitated the ruling body of a peaceable kingdom and was now getting their heads staked and ready for a victory parade.

There were too many animals in this room. It was getting on Dorothy's nerves.

Gaby looked at Dorothy.

Dorothy said, "What should we talk about?"

"You're not going to believe this," Gaby said, closing the door before taking a cross-legged seat on a large, unnaturally white sheepskin, "but I'm pregnant."

"I thought you guys were fighting," Dorothy heard herself say, looking down at the line of scalp that parted Gaby's hair. "I thought you weren't having sex."

"We're fighting but that doesn't mean we don't have sex," Gaby said. She reached an arm up and pulled Dorothy down to her level. "We always have sex. Do you not have sex?"

Dorothy tried to smile but it felt ghoulish, she could sense that her eyes were not participating, so instead she reached out and started rubbing Gaby's arm in a way that she hoped communicated camaraderie and joy but that she feared felt slightly lecherous.

"Of course," said Dorothy, unsure of whether she had just admitted to Gaby that she did or did not have sex. What did that mean, anyway, to "have sex," what kind of temporality did that phrase even suggest? It depended how far back and forward you cast the net, it was a question of averages, and there was a season for everything, as it said in the Bible, which meant that in a life of having sex there would be droughts of sexlessness, or would they be rains/reigns of sexlessness, and anyway, Dorothy didn't think that it was friendly, or tactful, to be so mathematical. This triumph of the quantitative was to be resisted. Wasn't that the point of literature?

"Congratulations," she remembered to say. "About your . . . conception."

She wanted to be light, casual, and instead had chosen a word that sounded unfortunately clinical. But what was she supposed to say? She didn't want to make the mistake of calling something a baby before someone else did. "That's so great," she added. "So great."

"No, no," said Gaby. "I'm not going to keep it."

Dorothy, who felt that the dramatic import of Gaby's statement permitted a concomitant physical response, let her hand drop from Gaby's arm, where it had been lingering too long; then she doubted her timing, realizing that it could be perceived as unfeminist to withdraw physical affection at the first expression of a nonmaternal urge, and put the hand back, gently, near the elbow, as a sign of solidarity and sisterhood. Then again, if Gaby did not need solidarity—if that in some way made the moment *more* dramatic than it should be, if Gaby believed—correctly!—that terminating a pregnancy was NBD and did not call for any special expressions of sympathy and support, then Dorothy would have been right to drop her hand. Fuck, she really did not know what to do with her hand. No wonder Gaby had smoked for so long.

"What does Brian say?" asked Dorothy.

"He says it's up to me," said Gaby, extricating her arm from Dorothy's hand in a casual way that suggested she appreciated the support but was done with it. Dorothy pretended to have an urgent itch on her head and scratched furiously, which had the effect of making her head actually itch. Gaby ducked her own head a little guiltily to the side, her eyes searching but searching inward, as if looking not at Dorothy but deeper inside her own psyche. She rapped a knuckle on her teeth. "What do you think?"

Before Dorothy could hazard a guess, Gaby was explaining, the words falling out of her mouth, absorbed and somehow muffled by the softness of the room, the stuffed animals, rug, blankets, upholstered furniture, and sheepskin acting as, if not a literal sound barrier, an emotional and psychological panic room. Brian, Gaby said, wanted to keep the baby. They intended to have another at some point—the marriage had been better ever since they "trained" Sherman to sleep, which had, it seemed, solidified their bond by uniting them against him, as well as helping Gaby's brain heal from the torture of sleep deprivation, although she admitted that there was something evilly neoliberal about the notion that a baby should learn to soothe himself, like *what had happened to care?* And *what was this obsession with self-reliance?*—and he felt that the pregnancy was some kind of sign or, more accurately, he was the kind of person who went with the bird in the hand rather than waiting—and here Gaby pointed to her crotch in a lewd gesture, the kind that she rarely made when sober but always did when drunk—on the bush. But while Gaby definitely wanted another baby "someday," she wasn't ready. She still felt postpartum. She did not want to be partum. She wanted to be prepartum, nonpartum, for as long as possible.

"My mom always said she wished she had waited longer to have me," said Dorothy.

"See?" said Gaby. "Maybe she should have."

"But then I wouldn't be me," said Dorothy. "I would be somebody else."

Gaby stared at her like she was assessing how seriously to take her. She rooted around in the toy bin and pulled out a wooden bus. Even the bus had a face. It was deranged, when you thought about it, this impulse to put a face on everything. "So you think I should have it?"

"No," said Dorothy. "I mean, I'm here. I'm already me. I'm just saying. This baby won't be that baby, of the future." She cringed. There it was: *baby*.

"I need my bodily autonomy," Gaby said grandly, words that seemed to come from an internal teleprompter or an article she had read online. And then, with bitterness: "I don't want to be some mammal reproducing constantly.

"Did you know," she said, spinning each wheel on the bus in turn, "that nursing whales produce two hundred liters of milk a *day*?"

Dorothy wasn't sure if she was supposed to answer this or not. But: "You told me that before," she said.

Gaby touched her breast and winced. "I have to go pump soon," she said. "Gross."

"How did you get pregnant while nursing?" asked Dorothy. "I thought that was impossible."

Gaby shrugged. "It happens. I'm just *incredibly* fertile, I guess. *Very* womanly." She tossed the bus into an open bin—it also had a face—and dropped her voice conspiratorially. "You know what's crazy? I haven't even gotten my period because of the breastfeeding. There was literally no period to skip. You know how I figured out I was pregnant?"

She leaned in closer and Dorothy involuntarily held her breath.

"I just felt it!" Gaby shouted, and fell on her side laughing. "Motherhood is nuts. I'm a fucking psychic now!" She covered her face like they were about to play peekaboo. Skulls and lightning bolts alternated on the perfect almonds of her nail beds.

"You didn't take a pregnancy test?" asked Dorothy.

"No, I took one later," Gaby said, deflated by the dull practicality of the question.

"When are you going in for the . . . procedure?" asked Dorothy. Using the word "abortion" felt taboo, even obscene, in part because of the infantile milieu in which they were ensconced but more because the word was overly precise or somehow gauche, like asking someone how much they paid in rent.

"I have to go to the clinic and get the drugs," said Gaby. "I'll do it next week."

"What are you waiting for?" Dorothy asked. "Don't you feel like you should do it soon?"

Gaby reached out and hugged Dorothy. "It's fine," she said. "I'm on it."

Gaby had the power to decide when she created life, and she also had the power to delay terminating it until a more convenient moment. She was a god of fertility and chronology. The law had made her thus. If the casual way she wielded her temporal majesty offended Dorothy, she also found it, objectively, admirable. The revolutionary power of feminism depended on convenience; you couldn't break the glass ceiling and cook a meal from scratch. Their mothers had struggled just so that one day Gaby could make her life convenient, so she could be free to arrange it as she wanted. Not Dorothy's actual mother, who was against abortion, except in cases of rape, incest, and where the mother's life was in jeopardy—but the women of the past, the general mothers who had made the world that they had inherited, where it was possible for them to wear pants, study science, open a bank account without a husband, etc.

"I can come over and help you," Dorothy said. "It's kind of stressful at home. You shouldn't be alone when you do it."

"How do you know?" Gaby said. She looked at Dorothy with something between suspicion and curiosity, like Dorothy was a most unusual specimen and Gaby was on the verge of an interesting discovery. For a moment Dorothy almost believed that Gaby could see everything, that she was, as she had attested, psychic, or at least intuitive.

Dorothy dragged her palm over the soft fur of the murdered

sheep's hide. The raft children would call them barbarians for decorating their nurseries and dens with the skins of mammals. As a display of power it was gratuitous; no one doubted that the sheep were not in charge. Then again, what was the substitute? A synthetic that did not biodegrade? Was sustainability barbarism?

"Hello," Gaby said, her hands wrestling each other in her lap. "How do you know what it's like?"

Dorothy wanted to tell her. But she did not want to shift the terms of the conversation from choice to contingency. She did not want Gaby to start feeling bad for her, to ask if Rog had been excited, to hold her hand and grieve. There was nothing to grieve. It was just another false start.

"Do we know someone who's done it at home?" Gaby pressed. "Who was it?"

"It was me," Dorothy said to the airplane mobile.

"You had an abortion?" Gaby asked. Her tone of disbelief cut Dorothy and emboldened her. Why was Gaby so surprised that she had had an abortion? She could have an abortion if she wanted! She could have an abortion just the same as anyone else! She had the right to control time and maternity!

"Yes," Dorothy lied. "I mean, a medication abortion. At home. Like you're going to do."

A pain she had barely been aware of subsided, and Dorothy felt the satisfaction of the late reveal: *I am a person with experiences of which you know nothing! I have depth and interiority!* Dorothy knew it was wrong to resent Gaby for not knowing things she hadn't told her, but she also knew that sometimes you resent someone for the wrongs they have done to you and sometimes you resent them for the wrongs you have done to them. Even though she didn't think that she had done anything wrong. Even though it felt like she had.

"When? Why didn't you tell me?" Gaby's eyes were cloudy, wounded.

Dorothy shrugged, helplessly, to herself. She felt herself swimming farther away from safety with no way to get back. What Dorothy was really telling Gaby was that while Gaby had come to her for help, Dorothy had, in the same situation, *not* gone to her for help. There was no way for Gaby not to understand this as some kind of judgment. But it was also true that no one should have to tell anyone everything; that isn't friendship, it's extortion. "I'm telling you now," she said.

"When? Whose was it? Rog's?" Gaby wanted to know.

"No," said Dorothy quickly, afraid of whatever karmic retribution would befall eliminating, even in the realm of language, another of Rog's unborn offspring. "Someone from before. A one-night stand. Do people still use that expression?" Now the lie involved a fictional character. Now it was attaining its own dimensionality, becoming more solid but also more slippery.

Gaby swatted Dorothy's arms. "Secrets!" She giggled. "Woman of mystery!"

Dorothy shrugged, affecting modesty. She could be sophisticated. A modern woman who went out and had abortions and didn't even need to talk about it.

"Were you okay?" Gaby asked, looking closely at her. The bracelets clinked as she played with her hair.

"It's a lot of blood," said Dorothy.

"No, I mean emotionally," said Gaby. "Are you okay with it now?"

"Of course," Dorothy said, remembering her lines. "I wasn't going to have a baby with a stranger."

"A stranger?" Gaby said. "Like you picked him up in a bar? That's not like you."

Before the deception could acquire an unmanageable degree of detail, Dorothy waved a hand. "He was a grad school person," she declared, forcing herself to look at Gaby, counting on how boring her nonacademic friends found everything to do with her institutional life. "Not a stranger-stranger." As predicted, Gaby lost interest in the imaginary father immediately.

"Wow, this is so cool," Gaby said. She gathered her hair into a nest on the top of her head. "That we will both have had abortions!"

There was something appealing about being the same as Gaby. It was sisterly, like sharing clothes—something they had never done.

Gaby paused, seeming to remember something.

"So all those times with Sherman when I was really sick in the mornings and saying to you, 'You'll see one day,'" Gaby said, "you already knew? How far along were you?"

"Not far," said Dorothy. "Ten weeks.

"And I didn't get nauseous," she lied.

This lie was easier to declare. It was like slapping a coat of paint on the walls of the lie to fix it up. Dorothy just had to remember what she was saying, in case she had to repeat herself later. *(1.) no nausea;(2.) a grad school person*—she could always say it was Keith. Dorothy's real experience of nauseated limbo was displaced and this new past—unqueasy, academic, decisive—took over. She felt a warm glow of pride, to have participated so completely in the exercise of her legal rights and the hard-won power to shape her own destiny. What good were rights, people said, if you didn't use them? Could you even call yourself a woman without undergoing this most critical reproductive rite of passage? On what foundation other than personal experience could politics be based? Principles? Principles were theoretical at best.

"ANYWAY," Gaby said, touching a breast and grimacing. She produced a portable pump out of nowhere and started unbuttoning her dress. From another nowhere came an empty bottle.

"Shouldn't you wash your hands first?" Dorothy asked.

"It's fine," said Gaby.

"Enough about our wombs," she added as the milk gushed into the bottle. "What else is new with you?"

"I have to go to the bathroom," said Dorothy.

The bathroom smelled like a restaurant bathroom. Ferns hung from the ceiling and a candle was burning on the back of the toilet. Dorothy raised it above her head gingerly, careful not to spill the wax, to read the bottom. Eucalyptus.

Dorothy would have anticipated feeling guilty about lying to Gaby, but in fact she felt relieved. A version of the truth had come out—Gaby now knew that Dorothy had once evacuated the contents of her uterus at home. It was good that she knew. It was like putting an exhibit into evidence. But the version the court had was distinct enough from the truth that Dorothy did not feel she had lost anything or given it away. She had kept herself to herself.

She turned off the overhead light to better soak up the atmosphere of the candle. She unzipped her pants and sat on the toilet. There was a shadow or stain on the cotton of her underwear so she reached her arm over to the switch and turned the light back on. The tampon was soaked to the string and some blood had gotten on her underwear. It was her regular period. It had returned yesterday. Things would be normal now. She was passing an unfertilized egg, unimplanted uterine lining. The time of the blight was no more. She peed, and the cotton bundle dislodged a little, pushing itself out. She pulled on the string, formerly a pale blue. The wad of cotton came out a winey purplish brown, like a bruise or rotting fruit, and soaked to a gloss. For a moment the tampon bobbed from the string like a dead fish and Dorothy hastened to wrap it in paper before it dripped on the toilet seat or her clothes.

The forty-dollar hand soap smelled like cedar. Dorothy hoped her casket would smell this good. She washed her hands twice and took a black plastic comb from her bag and combed her hair. Brown hairs filled the sink, fluffy and rising. She swirled them together with a little water, then swirled the wet, matted hair mass over the hair that had fallen to the floor and threw it all away. One recalcitrant strand floated up and worked its way down the side of the trash can; Dorothy wrapped it tight around her finger and pushed the coil off. She used a square of toilet paper to tamp down the trash and left it there, like a blanket for the hair ball.

Yellowish plaque was clinging to the spaces between the comb's teeth. Compressed skin cells, hair product, scalp oils. It looked waxy, aural. Using her fingernails Dorothy dug out the wax and pushed it through the short plastic teeth. She washed her hands again, careful to scrape under her fingernails. She rinsed the comb and dried it with the hand towel.

The party had gotten louder since Dorothy had been in the bathroom. More guests had arrived, or people who had been floating around in other rooms or smoking outside on the fire escape had come back. Dorothy squeezed behind a cluster of Gaby's friends who she knew from years of Gaby events to reach a hand into the bowl of baby carrots. It was a bamboo bowl and less sturdy than it looked; she almost knocked it over but the bowl wobbled on its axis and righted itself. She ate the carrot, and another, breathing in the apartment like air. The secretary desk. The ten-thousand-dollar sofa. She knew what it cost because Gaby had told her what a great deal they got on it—it was actually worth more. The built-in bookshelves. Art by actual artists, friends who gave it to Gaby when she, of all people, could have afforded to pay for it. Brass objects arranged on a shiny chrome table like a hotel lobby. The drinks and mixers were on a long table protected with a tapestry Gaby had dyed herself. Dorothy poured herself a vodka with a dash of tonic and looked around for a lime. There was no lime.

Gaby lived in a million-dollar apartment and was going to give herself an abortion on a sofa that cost four months of Dorothy's rent and Dorothy was supposed to put a lemon in her drink. *What the fuck,* thought Dorothy, and squeezed the lemon in. Seeds floated to the bottom of the cloudy cup.

An immigration rights attorney who Dorothy had not seen since Gaby's baby shower was talking about her two-year-old son.

"Sometimes when he puts his face right next to mine I have the urge to French him," the attorney said, raising her voice to be heard over the music. Her tone was confessional but the rapid way in which she delivered the confession made Dorothy think it was not a true confession, compelled to surface in the imperfect moment, but a line that had been worked over and tested in front of smaller, more familiar audiences, before being rolled out on this festive occasion. "Do you guys think I'm a pedophile?"

A man with an athletic build and a square superhero jaw-line who was a partner in a litigation finance firm said, "If you really thought you were a pedophile, you'd never make a joke about it."

The woman, the immigration rights attorney, shrugged. "I have thoughts," she said.

"You're bragging," the litigation financier said again. He had a trendy haircut. His shoes, brown leather with laces and a peppy little heel, looked new. His face was sweaty with the effort of repartee but he stood perfectly still. He didn't hop a little from side to side. He didn't scratch himself or touch his hair. But he seemed to be working very hard not to do these things. There was something vibrating beneath the surface.

"It's very romantic," the woman insisted. "I know what a vibe is."

"Excuse me," said Dorothy, although she had not really been part of the conversation, and pushed her way to the kitchen. She needed water. She was bent over in the refrigerator, reaching for the bottle of seltzer, located inconveniently behind a gallon of milk, when she sensed the intrusion of some male presence. She closed the refrigerator and turned around. Rog. He asked how it was in the baby's room, and looked concerned, like he thought Dorothy might start crying, and bawl her regrets, or worse, insist that they try again, although "again" wouldn't be accurate, since they hadn't been trying in the first place.

"It was cool," she said, and not seeing any cups, took a swig from the bottle, a liberty she felt, as Gaby's best friend, entitled to take.

"Are you sure?" Rog asked, handing her a cup.

"Definitely," said Dorothy. "Thanks."

She poured some more seltzer into the cup and drank again. Her reasons for not telling Rog about Gaby's situation had less to do with protecting Gaby's privacy than not wanting to get dragged into a conversation where she would wind up admitting that she had lied. Not that he would necessarily chastise her. He might like that she had kept their secret for just them. It might make him feel closer to her, like they had a thing no one else had. But she didn't want to get into it right now. Right now they were at a party.

Nestling the bottle of seltzer against her chest and holding the cup in front of her like a flashlight she followed Rog back into the living room, where they rejoined a cluster of people he had been talking to. The water was helping, lightening the vodka headache before it settled too deeply into her brow. In a deep bass voice, a man with a black beard was saying excitedly, "But that's not what fascism *means*." He was paunchy, and even though he did not look like any dentist Dorothy had ever visited, she could not shake the notion that he could or should be a dentist. Perhaps it was because his own teeth were so white and orderly, lined up like soldiers for inspection. His wide, bear-like hand was precisely shaped to hold a drill.

Dorothy and Rog chatted with him until he looked over Dorothy's head at something behind her. "I should go mingle," he said, and walked away.

The music changed, from folky melodies to hip-hop, and the energy of the party coalesced around this new, more insistent shape. There was an empty chair and Dorothy dropped into it. It was curved and cherry red and covered in some soft twill fabric, and she felt enveloped, like she was in a cove. She couldn't begin to guess what it cost.

Gaby popped up from—where? The floor?

"You found the womb chair," she said. "That's what it's called."

"Oh," Dorothy said.

Gaby raised an eyebrow at Dorothy. *Womb chair,* she mouthed again, and there was some new aggression there, a flash of claws. Dorothy didn't think Gaby was on to her lie, but it occurred to her that maybe Gaby hadn't really been happy to learn about Dorothy's fake abortion. Maybe Gaby's acting like they had something in common was her way of dealing with the disappointment of feeling less special and singular, of having to share her abortion spotlight. Maybe she had been really excited to tell Dorothy her news. Maybe that was why Dorothy had lied in the first place—not to help her, but to take something away from her. Like Elyse had said, no friendship is free from competition. Nothing was. They lived and died in an economy of scarcity. That was the way of the world. When someone has everything, even if you love them, you sometimes wish that they had a little less.

"My mother-in-law bought this book," Gaby said, in the faraway voice of alcohol, as if they were in the middle of a different conversation, "for the baby."

"Oh yeah?" Rog said politely, without looking up from his phone, from his position behind the chair.

"It's about a bear. It's about all the fun stuff the bear does in different seasons," Gaby said. "He ice-skates in the winter, sings in the rain. You know, spring. But I feel like such a fraud reading this book. Why am I teaching him about the seasons? We don't have seasons anymore."

"It sounds like Bear is a good role model," Rog said, putting his phone back in his pocket. "Like he makes the best of any weather."

"Maybe I should assign it to my Apocalypse class," said Dorothy. "They love talking about the weather. Do you want to come in and do a presentation?"

"Ha, ha," said Gaby. "You don't understand." She dragged herself to her knees, put her hands on the top of her head. "I'm engaging in an act of *deceit*. I'm preparing him for a world that will never be again."

"Don't you think that's what all parents do?" asked Dorothy. "Raise kids equipped to handle the childhood they had? In correcting one set of mistakes you make entirely new ones.

"Or," she said, seeing the frown that indicated that Gaby didn't like Dorothy, who had no children, who was, as far as Gaby was concerned, child-free by choice, theorizing on her turf, "it's like reading Plato so you can read Heidegger's critique." She couldn't suppress the little smile that crawled across her face whenever she showed what she knew. "He has to know the rules so he can understand what it means to subvert them."

"If you say so," said Gaby, who didn't get the reference and didn't care. "But there's this page in the back that talks about spring, summer, autumn, winter. It shows, you know, snow falling and the leaves turning red. Why does he need to learn this stuff? It's just confusing."

It was like Gaby to call something confusing rather than depressing—as if there were a better way to present the facts, as if that would change how you felt about them.

"Just pretend you live in L.A.," said Rog. "We never had snowmen there."

Around midnight, Rog nudged Dorothy and cocked his head. Gaby was hauling out a karaoke machine. The sight of the machine filled Dorothy with dread.

"Shit," she said.

For a long time she had loved karaoke. Honestly, she had loved it too much. The love was frantic but also complex, a complexity born of her desire to expose herself and be known, and her concomitant dread of exposing herself and being known. Of all the forms this conflict had ever taken in her life, karaoke was the purest.

"Do you want to leave while we still can?" Rog asked.

"Yes," Dorothy said, "but I think it's too late." Gaby was plugging wires into the TV with calm efficiency, a modern-day Hans Castorp "running" the gramophone in the sanitarium salon.

They used to do it in private rooms. At first it had all been so new and enchanting: the sticky darkness; the bizarre accompanying videos, about which someone always had something to say; the caterwauling audible from inside the bathroom, when the nights other people were passing in other private rooms leaked into your own; and all this inside the dark and deep alcohol cocoon. Inside this cocoon her voice was so good, so strong. It was amplified and loud enough to fill her head. Her friends, and their friends, were so beautiful. She could see their souls shining; it was an unbearable burden, to love them so much.

The problem with karaoke in those years was that it was so hard for it to end, and sometimes, depending on what kind of liquor she was drinking, in the later/earlier hours of the morning Dorothy became morose, or fell into a funk as dark and soft as dirt. She might rouse herself out of it if someone encouraged her to sing again, or she might keep falling if someone started to sing a melancholy song. There was a variety of funk that Dorothy liked settling into, aided by nostalgic songs, when she felt the fragility of her ebbing youth and the sweet ache of pleasures she had known or missed; there was another funk that was loneliness and grief, and sometimes these two funks blended together into an overpowering pang of life and death in which Dorothy experienced the smallness of her being knit into the large, incomprehensible whole of everything else. Great passions were expressed and mourned. She would come home wound up like a clock, pulsing with all the songs sung and unsung, running on anxiety and regret, amped up and disappointed, wanting more and also wanting to have had much less.

That, too, was part of the love—the bitterness that it did not last.

Some time ago karaoke had stopped being fun, and then it had become a chore, and then a kind of poison that caused Dorothy's internal organs to shut down one by one, but still she did it—sometimes it was even her idea. It was hard to stop doing something you had once liked doing. There always seemed to be the possibility you could like it again. Could be the person you had been, who was now a stranger.

Gaby handed Dorothy the second microphone and put on an emotive ballad from their parents' youth. It was way too early to go full throttle on this kind of thing, but it was part of Gaby's charm that she never took the temperature of the room. Everyone else was engaged in cross talk or looking at their phones or, worse, a few people were staring at them, their heads idly nodding, offering half-smiles of polite encouragement. Dorothy felt that they were all prisoners together, but of what, she couldn't say—the dictate to enjoy? Nostalgia for a time they had never known? The obligation to please the hostess? Their own mortality? Their parents' mortality?

Gaby told Dorothy to stay up for the second number. It started loud and fast and high, and from the excitement in the room Dorothy gathered that this was a new song from a teen star that everyone except her had heard dozens of times and liked for reasons whose irony and sincerity could not be teased apart. Dorothy quickly passed the microphone to someone else.

"I've never heard this song before!" she shouted to Gaby, who was already belting the chorus. Listening to Gaby, Dorothy felt herself expanding and also felt the reflected glow of nobility that always attended the admiration of a friend. Love for someone else's karaoke performance was greater and more intense than love for a great song because it was love for the person singing. Karaoke involved destroying something significant and putting oneself into the place of the thing you had killed. Beautiful singing took you somewhere, it transported you in a reverie, but it took you back to yourself—that was why people cried when they listened to beautiful music. Amateurism kept the focus on the amateur. It was about appreciating the artist, not the art.

Karaoke doubled the song. Even when you didn't know the original song, you never heard just the version that was present; you were always aware of another version, a real version, a ghost version, to which the current version existed in relation. That was the pathos of karaoke. It was a way of striving, an imitation not in the cheap sense, but in the sense of the meaning that attends an imitation of God. There were, of course, people who put on joke songs and tried to distance themselves from the power, and Dorothy always felt sorry for them. *We are all in the gutter,* she always wanted to tell them, *but some of us are looking at the stars.*

The next drink Dorothy made tasted like metal, so she dumped it into the sink and opened a Tecate. The lawyer who had bragged earlier about wanting to kiss her toddler came into the kitchen and leaned against the counter. The lawyer was fully drunk now and feeling introspective.

"I was telling this guy out there," she said, "about my kid's tantrums. He didn't understand at all."

Dorothy drank the beer and ran her finger over the bottom of a glass bowl, picking up popcorn detritus. She could hear, from the other room, a group sing-along to "Wuthering Heights." It sounded like feral cats being raped—in a fun way. Dorothy licked salt off her finger. She burped into her hand and smiled to encourage the lawyer to keep talking.

"The other day I asked him if he wanted cinnamon and honey in his milk and he said yes," the lawyer said. "Why did I believe him? What the fuck does he know? I gave him the cup and he screamed for twenty-five minutes. It was like he was possessed."

Dorothy said that sounded very hard. The lawyer put a hand on Dorothy's arm.

"You get it," she said.

"Later on I figured it out," the woman said. "I remembered that when we got home, his stuffed monkey was sitting in his high chair. Of course *I* hadn't put the monkey there. *He* had put the monkey there, the night before, at dinnertime, and he had taken my seat, and I had sat in the place we usually pile bags. But when he came home from school, he saw the monkey in the chair and just lost his mind. He took him down and beat him against the table legs, saying, 'Push Alex.' I don't know if he felt replaced by Alex, or what. Maybe he was pushing Alex because he really wanted to push me. Then I gave him the tainted milk. I think he didn't feel seen." She said it again, her cheeks flushed with drinking and exhaustion and the heat of the party. "I think the milk made him feel unseen."

"I'm sure you handled it fine," said Dorothy, who, despite everything, really liked this woman. She had a way of telling a story. She was probably a good lawyer for her clients. And then, there was something so relaxing about being around a talker. All you had to do was keep them going. "Alex calmed down eventually, didn't he?"

"Alex is the monkey," the woman said.

"Right," said Dorothy, and Rog came in to say that Gaby wanted her back.

Gaby was handing out books with the song titles. She was a charming master of ceremonies, "dispenser of the entertainment" as well as star performer, cheerleader, and claqueur. A lesser host would have scratched the "wonder-box" with carelessness, would have turned up the echo to distorting levels. Some people Dorothy didn't know performed anthems that Dorothy herself had performed many times at karaokes past and Dorothy got no pleasure from them at all. A flat meanness had moved into the atmosphere; the fun was rote, spoiled. People got up and risked themselves for the group and no one acknowledged or even watched them. Maybe that was the point; there was a tact or politeness to ignoring the spectacle that they were all purportedly gathered to enjoy. In the ancient past people had gathered around campfires to sing together and blend their voices but now, a ritual that was ostensibly revealing or cathartic enforced a zone of untouchable privacy. And yet unlike the solitude that Dorothy knew was a good thing, the best thing, this privacy was only attainable in the act of exposure; as soon as the singers retired from the impromptu stage, the clearing of couches and tables, they were expected to drop their aesthetic and spiritual ambitions, to act as if they had never been in the clearing, tunelessly or tunefully reaching for transcendence.

Holding the microphone away from her lips to avoid popping, Gaby commanded Dorothy to put in a song. As Rog strolled through a crowd-pleasing version of the Pet Shop

Boys, Dorothy consulted the book and keyed in a numerical code. Someone got up and did a morose Smiths number that Dorothy wished she had thought of doing. The litigation financier accompanied his rendition of "Lola" with a staccato marchlike dance. Dorothy wondered if he danced this dance to all songs or if he was trying to communicate something specific about the sexual panic of "Lola." While the financier desperately punched the air Rog put his mouth over Dorothy's ear to be heard over the music.

"He seems so angry," Rog shouted.

"This song reminds me of that frat kid from Kansas," she answered. "Do you think that kid knows this song?"

Rog nodded but Dorothy wasn't sure he had heard her. A trio of women Dorothy had never liked came up to do a song from the nineties that Dorothy had never cared about, but she smiled and clapped, reluctant to diminish the experience for those who were provoked and moved by it. A woman in a sweater so loud it was chaotic briefly cleared the room with a frightening rendition of "Heart-Shaped Box." Alex's mom came in and did a disturbingly on-key Mariah Carey. People had secret talents; it thrilled Dorothy to be in their presence. After Gaby's next song Dorothy started thinking there might have been something wrong with the karaoke machine, which was essentially a children's toy. The sound had gotten tinny, like it was trapped inside something too small for it, but no one else seemed bothered or even to notice.

When her song came up, Dorothy didn't recognize the opening drumbeat, and although the melody announced itself, she couldn't find her way into it. It seemed to have no relation to the background pulsing of the synthesizer. She tried talking along with the words onscreen, but didn't recognize any of them, and even though Gaby sat at her feet, singing along to keep Dorothy on track, midway through the second verse Dorothy pushed the button to skip. A few peopled booed cheerfully.

"I'm sorry, I don't know this song!" she said. "I thought it was a different song!"

She made a hapless gesture that she hoped made her neurosis seem charming, like she was a character in an independent film—the kind who wears a hat.

Gaby scrambled up and put an arm around her.

"Give it up for Dorothy!" she said.

"I'm next," she added.

Gaby fixed her dress and did a little bow in front of the karaoke machine, summoning and supplicating its gods to her side. The percussion clicked quickly, on the run from something or someone.

"This is a classic," Gaby intoned into the microphone, and pointed at Dorothy. "Also by the Boss."

The synth came chugging on the drums' heels, and Gaby was right there on the beat. She dipped low into the melody. She knew every inch of the song, where it curved and where it rode straight. Brian, who Dorothy had not seen the entire night, materialized and grinned with the unmistakable pleasure of watching the person you love do something they excel at. Gaby raised a fist in a pantomime of the motion a singer makes onstage in front of hundreds of thousands but the way Gaby did it expressed her knowledge that she was in her own living room entertaining a handful of diehards and drunks who hadn't drifted away into other conversations, and happy to be there. If Dorothy still loved karaoke she would be falling in love with Gaby all over again, but she didn't. Dorothy was in her bathysphere, and Gaby was in her stadium.

"I'm just a lonely pilgrim, I walk this world in wealth," Gaby crooned. *"I want to know if it's you I don't trust. 'Cause I damn sure don't trust myself."*

What was the world behind the song, Hans Castorp had asked, *which the motions of his conscience made to seem a world of forbidden love?*

The answer was death. It was always death. There was no other song, really. The variety of earthly music was merely a reflection of the infinite ways there were to die. There were love songs, of course, but since love could kill you, they counted as death songs, too. The particular genius of this song was how fast it moved. It hurried like it was late to its own funeral.

Gaby's lip snarled imitatively. She was cute, like a lap dog. *"So when you look at me,"* she sang. *"You better look hard and look twice. Is that me, baby, or just a brilliant disguise?"*

Dorothy leaned into Rog.

"That was the song I meant to do," she said. "I put in the wrong one."

"This is a great song," he said.

From behind them a guy Dorothy had always hated for being such a sloppy drunk started whooping. "She's killing it!" he yelled, and Dorothy had to admit that she was. She imagined Gaby holding the song down with one hand and beating it in the face with the other until the song relented.

The lines of words fled from the screen, replaced, in a fair trade, with Gaby's voice, straining for power. Dorothy had been embarrassed by her mistake but now she saw that there was no reason to be embarrassed. It was good that Gaby had done the song, Dorothy decided. It didn't have to be her who did what could be done so well by someone else.

There was a printer in the department office she could have used, but Dorothy always printed in the library. Partly this was because she was always *in* the library and it seemed like the time wasted trekking over to the office was worth the money she spent on the print card, and partly it was because the minutes Dorothy had to spend standing by the office printer, waiting for it to print, were torturous. At any moment a professor from the department might come out and find her there, and accuse her, as had happened on two prior occasions, of being a student. Nor did she like the feeling that the secretary was keeping track of how much or what she was printing. It wasn't anybody's business what Dorothy did on the printers.

She got twenty free pages a week, anyway, so she sent the document from her laptop to the print queue, and, leaving her laptop open on the table, she crossed the library to the printer station, where, keeping one eye on the laptop across the room, she typed her university ID and password into the user interface. A message popped up, stating that she had exceeded her weekly print quota. She went back to her table, rummaged through her bag, retrieved her credit card from her wallet, navigated to the university IT site, and put twenty dollars on her account. Then she hit Ctrl+P again and went back to the printer station. In the interim, a girl with a Roman nose and baby pigtails had occupied the printer station. She was printing something on two sides with a lot of images that was coming out at a very slow pace, so Dorothy went back to her laptop and sent her document to the other printer. That print station was farther away, so this time she took her laptop with her, holding it open as she walked, though she left her coat and books and wallet behind. When she selected her job and entered her password, a message popped up saying that the printer was not able to print.

She looked at it. A large black plastic machine. Inscrutable. It looked like a filing cabinet attached to a calculator. A handwritten note taped to the outside warned users from powering down, so she popped open the tray without turning it off.

No visible jam.

No one was working at the librarians' desk, which didn't matter, because typically the librarians weren't very helpful about printer issues; their advice was always to try another printer in a different part of the library. If that failed they would send you to another library altogether. Their philosophy seemed to be that if no one used the printer for an unspecified amount of time, eventually the printer would sort itself out and get up and running again. Wait and do nothing: This was the kind of advice Dorothy was basically sympathetic to. That meant that she didn't need to take it, because she could give it to herself.

She tried hitting the printer. Not too hard; not hard enough to draw attention. Just a firm tap. The machine turned itself off.

This was exactly what she had been talking about with her first therapist that morning.

"It's not only the institution that's against me," she had said. "It's all the stuff in it. It's like whatever I touch malfunctions."

The therapist had nodded and furrowed her brows to signal that she heard Dorothy but did not agree with her interpretation.

"I make garbage," Dorothy had said.

"That sounds like self-blame," the therapist had said, mildly.

Outside the window: magnolia trees that had bloomed early and were now frost-covered. Inside the office: figurines, statuettes, a menagerie of urns and finger bowls, some pottery. Of course the therapist couldn't understand what she meant. There was nothing in here that even plugged in.

The main computer lab was down on the ground floor of the library. Dorothy, conscious of energy waste, took the stairs. The lab was a U-shaped ring of desktop computers under yellow fluorescence, rather like a corporate business center. A few kids were playing video games, with headphones. Others were typing. Dorothy logged on to a desktop computer next to a student playing a first-person racing game. The asphalt zoomed up like a tidal wave, curving back and forth under a blue sky scattered with puffy clouds. Dorothy tried not to look at the game screen because doing so made her carsick, but the vertiginous rise and fall of the road in her peripheral vision pulled her back. No wonder her students didn't do the reading. How could reading compete with this addictive sensation of nausea?

She located her document in the cloud and sent it to the printer in the lab. She walked over to that printer and entered her password. The high whine of the printer started up and died. The printer was out of paper. She checked the clock on the wall and decided that now would be a good time to go out for a few minutes to collect herself and buy a can of motor oil so she could come back and burn the library down.

There were reams of paper stacked up by the printer. Dorothy messily tore one open and began loading the paper in the tray. Her therapist had directed her to think about all the things in her life that did work. She paused loading the paper to check her email on her phone, which had the effect of summoning a gray-haired librarian. Just looking at her green sweater made Dorothy itch.

"Students aren't supposed to do that," she said.

"I'm a professor," said Dorothy. The claim, or having to make it, felt ridiculous. Of course the librarian didn't believe her. She didn't believe herself. She looked down at her clothes. They were shabby and studentish. Her hair was unwashed. She was probably shiny.

"Why are you printing here?" said the librarian. "You should print in your department office."

"Are professors not allowed in the library?" asked Dorothy. Her voice came out more sarcastic than she intended, and the librarian glared at her with actual contempt.

The university really did despise her. Just look at this librarian—a *librarian*! A *keeper of knowledge*!—and her ruthless face.

"That's a real question," Dorothy said. "I'd love to follow the rules, if only someone would tell me what they are."

The librarian took a step back, as if Dorothy were some subway lunatic. Her shrug said, *It's your life.* She removed a handful of paper—Dorothy had, typically, overdone it—and shut the printer tray door. She pushed a button to test. Efficiently the printer rolled out a sheet of hieroglyphics and bars of varying thicknesses.

"There," she said, like she had just wiped up some milk spilt from Dorothy's bottle. Dorothy looked into the future and saw herself, forty, forty-five years old, a contingent member of the faculty, waiting on the printers, absorbing the admonishment of the croney librarian, and thought how naïve she had once been to believe there was anything glamorous about the life of the mind.

Two undergraduates with buzzed haircuts were taking selfies in front of the bathroom mirror. Dorothy offered to take their picture together but they refused in such a way that indicated Dorothy's total miscomprehension of the scenario. Dorothy shut the stall door and locked it. There was a spot of red on her underwear. It was bright, like war paint.

The toilet seat was a little damp so she stood up and wiped herself and the seat and laid down two strips of dry paper. At the sinks the students were weighing the respective merits of socialism and communism. When Dorothy looked back at her own undergraduate conversations they seemed inane and juvenile, delusive, but these students made her feel hope, or maybe it was desperation. *The children will lead you,* she thought. *Oh God, please.*

She sat down on the covered toilet seat. Maybe, Dorothy thought, there was an abrasion in her vagina. A paper cut. She positioned her phone between her legs and took a photograph. The sound was all the way up and the camera made a loud shutter sound, as if film was advancing. The students continued to talk about the means of production. Because the flash had caused a garish bright spot that whited out the image, Dorothy touched through to the camera settings, turned off the flash, and took another photo. She zoomed in and moved around in the image.

No evidence of any surface tear or abrasion.

The blood must be coming from the inside.

This is my life now, Dorothy thought. *My life as a bleeder. I bleed between periods, or have one continuous period, that stops and starts after a few days, but the stops are not "stops," they are simply moments in the cycle—bleeding is the constant state.*

Her last period had ended after three days, and now this—whatever this was. The twenty-eight-day cycle had always been more a myth than a reality, a matter of averages or chemically enforced norms dressed up in lunar hocus-pocus, but there had been something coherent and reassuring about it. It was symbolic. Three weeks off, one week on. The week symbolized the creation, and destruction, of the world. The fact that the twenty-eight days existed as a myth or standard or average had made Dorothy feel that her body, or some statistical version of it, was connected to an axis ancient and foundational. But in the new era there were no symbols or organizing metaphors. The body was ruled by irregularity. All was chaos. In a time of chaos, one had to be prepared for everything. That was it: She had to prepare. She pushed the button to get to the home screen, touched the Notes application, and made a note:

Buy panty liners (pink individual wrappers)

Dorothy rooted around in the zippered bag she kept in her backpack, but all she came up with was a tampon. She didn't want to put in a tampon now. She wasn't sure how much blood was coming. There was always the risk of toxic shock. Also, she hadn't completely abandoned the hope of a surface tear.

Dorothy took out her phone again and looked at her email and then the news and then her email again. Danielle had sent a long message about the final paper but Dorothy didn't feel that it was appropriate to write to a student with her pants down. Danielle wouldn't know, of course, but *she* would know, and it would change how she interacted with Danielle in the future. It would be hard to shake the feeling that Danielle had seen her do it. It was one thing to read emails from students in bathroom stalls, but she could not be emailing students from bathroom stalls. It was important to fight the geographic creep of technology. It was important to do some tasks in some places, and other tasks in other places. *Dirt is matter out of place:* Mary Douglas.

She dabbed at the stain on her underwear with toilet paper to dry it; it was already mostly dry. She wrapped a piece of toilet paper three or four times around her underwear, looping it into an informal napkin, and pulled her pants back on. She flushed with her foot and used her elbow to bang open the stall door. It ricocheted against the neighboring stall. She ran her hands under the hot water and shook them under the dryer. One student was now sitting on the counter applying makeup. The other was talking on the phone. Whereas before they had seemed two members of some exclusive coven, now they acted like strangers. Dorothy let the door bang behind her.

Standing in the dim lobby, half-hidden by a marble statue of a dead founder, Dorothy opened the podcast app on her phone and thumbed in her second therapist's name. The icon showed the therapist smiling and wrapped in her usual shawl, in front of a brick wall. She was cut off at the shoulders. Two hundred and twenty-eight listeners had given her an average of five stars, but Dorothy knew you couldn't trust reviews. She scrolled down and clicked on "Episode 2.1: Precarity and Preparation." The therapist, whose voice sounded slower and smoothed out, like an audio engineer had taken a rolling pin to it, explained that this episode would feature an obsessive-compulsive barista who had gone into debt outfitting a doomsday cabin. Then a hissing white noise took over, transporting the listener into the windowless office that Dorothy knew so well.

Outside it was windy and some trash, a piece of wet paper, got stuck to Dorothy's knee; she peeled it off with her bare hand and it got stuck to her hand and then she flapped it off and it was gone. She raised the volume to hear over the squall of traffic. The subway was late and while the barista enumerated her latest bulk acquisitions and her recent purchase of a firearm, Dorothy researched the history of "obsessive-compulsive" in her phone's browser. A seventeenth-century bishop had identified obsessional thinking as a "scruple"—*trouble where the trouble is over, a doubt when doubts are resolved*. The nineteenth century had drawn a distinction between obsession, "in which insight is preserved," and delusion. The problem with the barista's situation, of course, was that it was impossible to say whether she was delusional or not. Things were definitely not okay in the world; the question was whether they were not okay in such a way that a cabin could make a difference.

The train car was crowded and Dorothy rode with her cheek against someone's green hiking pack, listening to the barista explain the sores on her hands, which were obviously chapped from repeated washing, as an allergic reaction. When the therapist began explaining the meaning of ego defenses, Dorothy hit Pause and took out her earbuds. The problem with the show, Dorothy was realizing, was that unless you got extremely lucky and someone happened to achieve a cathartic breakthrough on the day you were recording, most of the episodes were guaranteed to fumble or amble toward nonconclusion. What she had heard hadn't even offered the satisfaction of gawping; the anxiety was too ordinary, even if the manifestation was extreme. (Who *wasn't* preparing for the end of the world?) It didn't seem like that could be the point of the show—to faithfully document an ordinary suffering interiority with no expectation of event or transformation and the barest glimmer of insight—but if it wasn't, Dorothy had no idea what the point was.

At Gaby's stop, the man sitting beneath Dorothy (she was holding on to the bar above), made a move as if he wanted to get up. He was a half-century old, Caucasian, in a baggy suit; when she stepped back to let him pass, he slid his hand around her waist.

"Don't touch me," Dorothy shouted, and the man slipped past and disappeared. Everyone looked at her, then quickly looked away. She pushed out the door and saw a group of teens farther down the track horsing around near the yellow line. After the train pulled away, one of them dropped or threw a soda onto the tracks, and Dorothy averted her eyes from what she feared could be an imminent tragedy and jogged up the stairs into the bright light.

The temperature had risen ten degrees since the morning and Dorothy stripped off her cardigan while she walked. It was three o'clock and the sun was still strong. Dorothy thought it was strange that Gaby didn't want to wait until Brian came home to take the misoprostol, but she had told him it was "female business," and though his feelings were hurt, he was ultimately fine with it. It was her body and her choice. "He and I have talked a lot about Sherman's birth," she had explained over the phone. "I was glad he was there, of course, and I know that he had to be, but in another way it would have been better without him, with just me and the midwife and the doula." When Dorothy asked how it would have been better, Gaby said, "Witchier."

If witchy was what Gaby was going for, Dorothy didn't think they should be terminating her pregnancy in the afternoon. It was too healthy, too sanitized a time of day—like Gaby was violating some essential twilight prerequisite necessary to the ingestion of substances and the mystical powers of creation and destruction. Maybe Gaby was just more in touch with the bureaucratic nature of the event, the essential rightness of its occurrence during routine business hours. It wasn't like a clinic would let you schedule a D&C for nine P.M. Gaby answered the door in a red sweatsuit that was more expensive and flattering than Dorothy's fancy dresses. "It's my abortion outfit!" she announced.

There were piles everywhere: papers, books, dry goods that hadn't found their way into one of many cupboards, folded laundry leaning with the effort of waiting to be put away. Being rich did not make people tidy. In the kitchen Dorothy related how she had been groped on the subway after listening to her second therapist's podcast and Gaby dug around to find the instructions the clinic had provided her.

"Oh, I listened to it, too!" said Gaby. "I've been dying to talk about it with you."

It annoyed Dorothy that Gaby had listened to the podcast before she had, but she couldn't deny that she welcomed the opportunity to pick it apart with someone. "What did you think?"

Gaby pursed her lips like she was going to defer to Dorothy to speak first, and then charged headlong into opinion. "I didn't like the intro music," she said. "But I liked what she said about the stages of life. I don't think I ever successfully navigated initiative versus guilt. I think that's why I lack purpose in my career."

"What are you talking about?" asked Dorothy.

"Erik Erikson's third stage of development?" said Gaby. "The first episode of the podcast?"

"The first episode is a session with an obsessive-compulsive prepper," said Dorothy.

"Are you sure?" said Gaby.

"I think you listened to the wrong podcast," said Dorothy. "Do you even know my therapist's name?"

"How could I, when you never tell me," said Gaby.

A pause.

"Will you tell me?"

"Later," Dorothy lied, not wanting to start a fight, considering what they were gathered to do.

"We can listen to it *together,*" suggested Gaby. "While we're waiting for the contractions to begin."

"I think you should just take the medication," said Dorothy.

"I took it an hour ago," Gaby said. "It tasted like chalk."

It was like Gaby to not follow directions.

"You're supposed to put it in your vagina," Dorothy said. Gaby shook her head. "Look at the picture," she said, pointing to an illustration of an open mouth and a pill lodged under the tongue. Dorothy shrugged. Whatever authority she had in the situation was slipping away. "I guess you can do it both ways," she said.

A cry came from down the hall and Gaby excused herself. When she came back, she was holding Sherman. His face had gotten significantly fatter since Dorothy had last seen him—he was in a full-on Winston Churchill phase—and he was wearing a shirt with a collar and real buttons. Something about the buttons indicated to Dorothy that Gaby's priorities were not in order, that whatever she might say about the good motherhood had done her, she was fundamentally spinning her wheels, playing dress-up with a doll, spending hours of each day buttoning and unbuttoning clothes for a creature who was pre-verbal, whose greatest happiness was a successful poop.

"Jowly," said Dorothy.

"I swear he just winked at me," Gaby said. "I think he knows."

She went over to the shelf of records, Sherman in arms. "I feel like we need to pick the music very carefully," she said. "It's like losing your virginity, or waiting for the acid to hit." She scanned the shelf for a long time, at last selecting a Joni Mitchell album, then settled into the womb chair.

"This music puts me in touch with our foremothers," she said. "I bet this is what they listened to."

"They didn't have record players in back alleys," Dorothy said. The words sounded more pedantic than she had intended. She had intended to be arch.

Bouncing Sherman on her knee, Gaby launched into a long story about a time her mother had taken her to a carousel at a park in Napa while they were visiting her grandparents. "It's one of my earliest memories," she said. "When the ride started, the music was so loud that I started crying, but the guy in charge of the ride wouldn't stop it to let me get off. My mom went up to him after and just *reamed* him out. Yelling. Cursing. I remember feeling scared of her but also safe, like she was this lioness who was going to rip off the head of a rhino or whatever to protect me.

"But when I was talking to her the other day," Gaby went on, "she said that it never happened. That she took me to the carousel once, but that I didn't cry at all. Then she sent me a photo of her and me on the carousel. And I'm laughing."

The other thing, Gaby went on to say, was that in the photo, she wasn't wearing what she remembered. "In the photo I'm wearing this ridiculous pinafore," she said, "but I remember wearing a sailor suit—also ridiculous, but not the same."

"Are you sure?" said Dorothy.

Gaby put her glasses on top of her head and rubbed her face like she had an eraser in her hands. "Of course I'm not sure," she said.

"Maybe there was another time," said Dorothy. "With a babysitter."

"You see what I'm saying," said Gaby. "Either I'm not me, or my mom isn't her. But one of us isn't who I think she is."

They sat in silence, listening to Joni Mitchell follow an aimless melody. Dorothy had always hated Joni Mitchell. It always seemed like it took Joni Mitchell too long to get to wherever she was going.

Gaby's mother had been angry with Gaby for misremembering. "She said that this is why children shouldn't complain about their parents," Gaby said. "Because they don't have all the facts."

Formerly Gaby would have been irate at such a statement, but since becoming a mother herself she had begun to identify with her mother, to see her past from her mother's point of view rather than from her own. She said it was like seeing double. It annoyed Dorothy that Gaby had thrown over her own experience, and for such an obvious utility: By forgiving her mother so completely for whatever her mistakes had been, Gaby could preemptively excuse whatever ways she would fail Sherman. Reproduction, which advertised itself as remaking the future, instead had everything to do with revising and reconciling the past.

Gaby frowned while she chased the right words. "Waiting is not easy!" she finally said, laughing. "That's the title of one of Sherman's books. He's too young for it." Before Dorothy could say anything, Gaby grimaced. "I think I'm having a cramp," she said.

Dorothy had a strong urge to leave the apartment. "I can run to the drugstore and buy you a heating pad," she offered. Gaby told her there was one in the bathroom cabinet. Dorothy retrieved it and untangled the long white cord and plugged it in. It got hot very fast. Then she fetched Gaby a glass of water.

"Drink this," she said.

"Why?" asked Gaby.

"I don't know," said Dorothy. "Water is good for you."

Gaby drank. "Water is life," she said.

"Seriously," said Dorothy. "Can you think of one situation that wouldn't be improved with a glass of water?"

Gaby smiled but it was forced; Dorothy could see she wasn't feeling well. Dorothy took the glass to the kitchen and refilled it and came back. Sherman had fallen asleep in Gaby's arms and she handed him to Dorothy. He smelled delicious, like new bread. Dorothy had the strange sensation that she was a prince and Sherman a princess she wanted to carry across a threshold. She felt calm, but also frightened. Babies were so stupid. They had no judgment. They put their trust in anyone who came along.

Gaby turned on the television—she was the only person Dorothy knew who paid for cable—and found an old movie. They watched in silence for a few minutes.

"This doesn't feel traumatic," Gaby said.

"I didn't say it would be," said Dorothy.

"Shermie looks happy with you," said Gaby. "Did I ever tell you what he would do when he was first born? He would be trying to nurse, but he would cover my nipple and then bash his face against his own hand in a panic, like, *Where is it?*"

"The human condition," Dorothy said. Her shoulder was starting to hurt.

"I think so, too," said Gaby. She chewed her lip. Barbara Stanwyck had just appeared on the screen. "I miss that time. He was so tiny. Like a chicken, with his mouth always open."

Occasionally a grimace or look of consternation passed Gaby's face. Her eyes were hollowed with blue and the skin around her mouth looked puffier than usual, though whether that was due to the pregnancy or the stress or the general fatigue of maternity, Dorothy couldn't be sure. Then Gaby clutched the heating pad to her abdomen and breathed deeply and said, "I think it's starting." She went to the bathroom and came back. "No," she said. "Nothing."

Dorothy made a noise to indicate solidarity. On the TV Barbara Stanwyck was boarding a train for Palm Beach. Sherman was heavy and some drool was collecting around the corner of his mouth and Dorothy gently used his collar to wipe it away. She felt an ache travel down from her neck to her shoulder and through her arm. His trust was pure dead-weight. He breathed deeply, erupting occasionally into snores. He did sound like a seal. Gaby shuffled down the hall a little stooped over, exhaling through her mouth. Dorothy was gripped with the intense desire to look at her phone and find out what therapy podcast Gaby had stumbled across, but was afraid that if she got up Sherman would wake and see his mother doubled over in pain and be scarred for life and it would be her fault. So she sat there, not daring even to reach for the remote to lower the volume when the men on the train started shouting.

"Shhh," she whispered to Sherman. So consumed was she with shushing that she didn't hear Gaby shuffle back in.

"It got gnarly down there," Gaby announced. "But I don't have to tell you that.

"It's weird," she added. "This is the same drug they gave me when Sherman was born to *stop* the bleeding."

Dorothy asked if she wanted a pain reliever, but Gaby said she didn't need anything. "I can handle it," she said. "You know I didn't have an epidural."

Dorothy ignored this boast, which she had heard before, and asked if Gaby wanted to write down what time the bleeding had started.

"Just in case," she said.

"It's like you're my doula," Gaby joked. "But okay. Let's write it down."

At some point Gaby asked for the baby back. Sherman stretched his fists overhead and yawned and resettled against Gaby's body. She relaxed, like the air was going out of tires that had been close to popping.

"I feel like I can finally call myself a feminist," said Gaby, louder than Dorothy would have spoken with a baby in her arms.

"Take a picture of me," Gaby was saying, "I want to put my abortion on Instagram."

Dorothy looked over with a confused half-smile.

"Just kidding," Gaby said, moving Sherman from one arm to the other without disturbing his sleep, and rubbing her nose in his hair, "but it does sort of feel like the politics of having an abortion are lost if no one knows you had one."

Dorothy murmured something that could be taken for consent. She had thought Gaby would have more questions for her. She couldn't decide if she was relieved not to be interrogated or disappointed that Gaby didn't want to know more about what had happened to her. She knew this was inconsistent with her recent behavior and she did not care. She felt the need to be busier, to do something, to make herself indispensable rather than superfluous to the situation.

She got up and went to the kitchen and came back with a bag of pretzels.

"Eat something," she said, handing one to Gaby.

"Isn't it amazing," Gaby said, chewing the pretzel with her mouth open, insisting with her eyes that Dorothy agree, "that we have the power to *choose*?" Sure, she said, it had been exciting to be pregnant with Sherman, to be literally enormous with life and potentiality, and she had experienced the feminine capacity for reproduction in terms that can only be somewhat hokily characterized as a divine gift, but what she felt now, with her decision to terminate a pregnancy, was power, real, definite power—the power of choice. The choice to initiate something was not as meaningful, she said, as the choice to end it. Something beginning can mean anything. Something ending can only be what it's been.

"It's hard to know when something ends," Dorothy said.

"It's ending now," said Gaby. "I'm going to wake up tomorrow and give so much money to Planned Parenthood."

Before Dorothy left that night the bleeding had slowed considerably, and Sherman had been settled in his crib, the tinkling lullabies leaking from his room like the gentle soundtrack to the first act of a horror movie. At the door she warned Gaby that the bleeding might last longer than she anticipated. "They say ten days," she said, in her best performance of expertise, "but that's only an average."

At home that night Dorothy had one more stack of final exams to grade. After the end-of-semester speech she always gave her students in class, grading the last paper felt like staying too long at the party—saying goodbye and then having to awkwardly say goodbye again. So few of them in years past had bothered to pick up their finals that she had developed a policy of writing comments only if they dropped off a self-addressed stamped envelope in her office. But "where," they had complained, "are we supposed to buy stamps?" This year she had adjusted the policy. So long as they dropped off a self-addressed envelope, she would take care of the stamps. She didn't mind the post office. It put her in touch with an earlier phase of life: pen pals, lines, bells, and windows, Saturday morning errands with her mom. The post office was proof that you believed in the possibility of reaching someone, anyone. That a letter could arrive.

In the last week she had graded all her papers except those for the Apocalypse. *Saving the last for last,* she joked to no one, as she took the top sheaf off the pile. It was a paper on Samuel Beckett titled, "I Can't Go On, I Must Go On." *Not very imaginative,* Dorothy thought, and its author had not provided a self-addressed envelope. She skimmed the paper quickly and gave it an A-, placing it carefully into the small plastic trash can that she used as a recycling bin. She checked the headlines, and her bank balance, and the weather, and her email, and the headlines again. She clicked on a story about the border and read half.

The next paper in the pile was about Ulysses and the suitors. That, too, she skimmed, and gave an A-. Some professors railed against grade inflation, but Dorothy thought it was fine. No one was perfect, but near-perfection was the natural state of the human being. Made in the image of God, with some room to improve.

Previously when she had taught the class, Dorothy had insisted that they write papers on cultural objects that were strictly apocalyptic—about the literal destruction of Earth. But this semester Dorothy had taken a wider view.

"Every ending is an apocalypse," she had said on the last

day of class, then taken it back. "That's not true." But she had told them that they could write about any ending they wanted, anyway. Maybe the point of Writing Apocalypse was to get beyond the frame of the apocalyptic. Just make sure, she said, to explain how whatever ending you choose gives everything before it meaning.

"Actually," she said, glancing from the clock to their confused and insecure faces, "forget that." The idea that an ending gives what preceded it meaning was old. Time didn't work that way anymore. "Write about whatever you want," she had told them, "so long as it has something to do with the end."

"The end of what?" one sweet, stupid boy had asked.

"You tell me," she had answered.

He had chosen to write about the Paris Agreement, and included a self-addressed envelope. Dorothy put his work aside for tomorrow. Now was not a time for comments. It was a time for quick and dirty evaluation. Give them grades, move along. Render judgments. Send fires and floods and rainbows.

Next in the pile was a treatment of Freud's "Analysis Terminable and Interminable." It was good. A-. The next one was about the Puritans. It really deserved a B+, but Dorothy was in a groove: A-. The one underneath that was about Shiva. Enthusiastic A-! The one underneath that was about Banquo's ghost. It, too, came with an envelope. It, too, she put aside for tomorrow. Then came papers on genocide, coral reefs, the extinction of the dinosaurs, and the Roman Empire. There were three papers on the plague, two on the death of God, and one on the death of the novel. She felt a thrill spread like hot milk throughout her body as all the endings that had ever been piled up before her, and she graded them all the same, all nearly perfect, before dumping each one carefully, respectfully, into the trash.

Acknowledgments

Thanks to Chris Parris-Lamb, Alexis Washam, Sarah Bolling, Jillian Buckley, and Alicia Tatone. Thanks to Mark Lotto and Abby Kluchin. Thanks to Benjamin Nugent, Dana Hammer, David Levine, Rose Lichter-Marck, and Claire Lehmann. Thanks to Charles Petersen and the editorial staff of *n+1,* where the story "The Keeper" first appeared.

Thanks to my mother and father for everything, especially the babysitting.

Thank you, Gabe, for everything else: right down the line.

About the Author

Christine Smallwood is a contributing editor at *Harper's Magazine*. Her writing has
appeared in the *New York Times Magazine*,
The Paris Review, *n+1*, *Vice*, *The New
Yorker*, *Bookforum*, *T*, and many other
magazines. She has a PhD in English from
Columbia University. *The Life of the Mind*
is her first novel.